A lot of
life's
trivia

A lot of
life's
trivia

Ajayakumar Puthan Veettil

PARTRIDGE

A Penguin Random House Company

To order additional copies of this book, contact
Partridge India
000 800 10062 62
orders.india@partridgepublishing.com

www.partridgepublishing.com/india

CONTENTS

PRELUDE

'A lot of life's trivia 'is comprised of humorous stories of eager gentle men seek love secretly in the arms of their most fantasized women. The readers could almost feel all the characters in this book as curious next-door neighbors; some of them explore dreams and some may view as forbidden.

The main character, Mr. Johnson is a young, good looking Math professor. He is a married man, never seriously acquainted with other women except his wife. One day he receives a stupid phone call by an anonymous woman, inviting him to fulfill his clandestine, lustful fantasies. There's no denying the unique thrill of casual encounters! But, professor Johnson stumbles in to a series of blunders, even by ensuing voyeuristic opportunities!

Nancy, his wife, one day makes fun of him by conspiring a ridiculous incident, bringing him more excited at her friend Rachel. This incident drives him in to disillusionment and distracts him from his wife. Gradually, out of stupidity, he even resorts to seek out erotic adventure to Rachel. Here, Johnson's desire takes to another level, forgetting his unblemished service and obligation to his wife. He absurdly find his sexual arousal heightened by the luxuriousness of Rachel's elegance and openness.

Doctor David, on the other hand, is a widower, who accidently falls in love with a maid, which does not confirm the set ideals of a doctor. He succumbs to sexuality in his own private world,and indulge in a sinful relation, forgetting his age, and the aftermath of it. Finally, he get in to trouble, ensnared in a trap, demanding a huge prize of redemption. Then he seek out his friend, Johnson's help and find ways to free himself from the superfluous trappings. As a consequence, he breaks up norms and distort the true face of a sincere doctor. Doctor David's imbroglio brings light in to the sinister truth of lower middle class people's greed and blackmailing as well.

James is Professor Johnson's nephew, who falls in love with Doctor David's daughter, Sophia. He plays an exceptional role in the development of many events in the story.

The book is a bold narrative of the provocative facets of sexuality of the upper middle class gentlemen. The stories contained in the pages share a common thread, which bring light in to the sheer absurdities of urban gentlemen seeking out extra-marital relations and the ridiculous ways they find while fulfilling their sexual fantasies.

CHAPTER 1

THE TRYST THAT WENT RISIBLE

James entered the room and shoved the books on to the folding chair in the corner. His room was all crammy and the walls were of a mustard-yellow color which had in some places dings and scratches. Every nook and cranny were stuffed with books, papers and files. The Mahogany desk squatted in a corner was weary with an LCD monitor and accessories. James slid behind his desk and switched on his computer. Being out of town for some weeks had put him behind. He had so many summaries to prepare for the data base. Some minutes flew by as his fingers flew over the keyboard, entering required information in the data base. He was almost completing a month of on-site research for an article he was doing for a science magazine.

Just then his uncle came home. Barely five minutes after he walked through the door. James craned his head and turned to him with a broad smile.

"Good afternoon, James!"Mr. Johnson greeted from the doorway and went to a large window beside James. He looked out, wondering how James was faring for the past several days at his home. Then he straightened out with a weary sigh. He thought that, as each day went by,his concern for James grew, both for his wellbeing and for his reliability. Mr. Johnson, a college Math professor, was well aware that he had been spiriting his nephew away from the city for a special family week end in rustic seclusion to celebrate the beginning of their fourth year together. For all those days in the village, his nephew was winding his way along a seemingly endless country road, enjoying the hill station and the landscape, on either side of his motor bike. When he came fatigued, his aunt Nancy, a teacher at Lawrence residential school, was used to usher him inside after closing the front door. Then he could hear the sound of the thick iron latch that really matched the iron gate outside.

James was still busy, yet he could remember his aunt's profile with a tiny smile tugged at her lips as she loosened the pins at the nape of her neck. Then he could see her loose dark-brown hair slipped over her shoulders in a shimmering wave.

"I am going to arrange food, baby," She would say, spreading a huge plush towel on the bed beside him "You get upland just grab a shower".

James got on his feet as he saw his uncle reach in to the fridge. Mr. Johnson opened the fridge and pulled out a cold bottle of Sprite and locked the bottle opener under the cap. He flicked it off with a pop.

James, snapped his fingers with a loud laugh.

"Uncle, anything hot there?"

James went over to him as Mr. Johnson handed him a Knock-out beer. James opened the bottle hastily and clinked his against his uncle's before lifting it to his mouth. It was too icy cold as it slid down smooth his throat. The slow gulps of beer had a slightly inebriating effect on him. A feeling of lightness and pleasure flooded his brain and his whole body. On top of that, he felt the cool of the evening, which was gradually banishing the stuffiness of the day time. James turned to Johnson with a smile, threw back his head and sighed noisily. He passed a trembling hand over his forehead, and said blithely.

"What fun! Today I got a special mail". James leaned back against the wall with a muffled laughter, and folded his hands behind his head. He was thinking merrily about the mail! He wanted to see if the feeling in there was genuine or if it was just something conjured up by a naughty belle whom he hadn't seen so far.

What has she written! "I love you! You are my life, my happiness! James, I love your magnetic blue eyes and the slight cleft in your chin…I do not ask you to return my feelings! I only ask for your gracious presence in the old summer house out there at nine 'o' clock tomorrow morning. I think it's unnecessary to write my name. Please come…"

Although the mail didn't go deep in his mind, James smiled,feeling as if he's being baited. And he knew it. He was still suspecting that it was Sophia, the pretty chorus girl in the church. So many thoughts continued to drift in and out of his mind. He caught flashes of Sophia's wide- awake laughing face, as if she was purposely laughing so heartily and darting quick looks at him in the church. She was so beautiful with her well developed shoulders and exaggeratedly waspish waist. She was exquisitely dressed in a snug little denim skirt and a tight angora sweater on that day. She had the most incredible body, a fat and round chin with a perpetual smile on her lips. She's a creature so beautiful and wanton! And indeed, she was the continual subject of his sexual fantasies at the hill station.

"It's not love!," James murmured to himself, "One does not fall in love with strangers. I think it's just an amourette!"

Suddenly he remembered that the day before yesterday, while he was taking a stroll around in the fresh air at the churchyard, he met her unexpectedly. His nervousness was dissolved with an impish wink she threw at him as she went past him with her friends. Why did she brush past him with a wink and a lascivious smile?

"strange!". He wondered.

Johnson, who had given free rein to his thoughts, suddenly stopped pacing the room and turned to James. He studied his nephew's face for a moment.

"Something is in your mind, isn't it?" he asked,looking at him quizzically. James shrugged with a smile as if words would not come. Suddenly Nancy came in and stood a little way off from them. She scanned the room as if something tried her patience and kept frowning.

"See, what a mess is in here! James, your desk, the chairs, the walls and even the papers and books stacked in the corners are all covered up with dust. I need to re- arrange everything and brush off the last speck of dust......"Nancy mumbled.

As she looked intently, James could see her big face suddenly change, suffused with a bright red flush and smile.

A short while later, Johnson and Nancy went out of his room in to the corridor. Outside everything was hushed and the cold night was already enfolding the nature in its gentle, soporific embrace.

James lay down his canopy bed, pulled the blanket over his head,and closed his eyes. Slowly he dropped in to a profound sleep. In his deep slumber he had a sweet dream. He saw a pair of newlyweds stepping down the stairs of the church. Yet he was not sure whether the blurred image was he who was holding Sophia by the waist as she,in return, cuddled up to him! The newlyweds were so happy and rapturous. The morning sun looked down at them from behind the scraps of clouds and the air was thickly permeated with the fragrance of flowers.

Johnson and Nancy were living in an ancient mansion on the slope of Love Dale, five kilometre away from emerald lake in Nilgiri hills. It was a range of mountains with at least twenty four peaks above two thousand metres in the west-most part of Tamilnadu state. These peaks stood high on the larger part of the Western Ghats mountain chain, which made up the south-western edge of the deccan plateau. His old house had a spacious courtyard and the house was situated amidst huge columns of pine trees standing sentinel on either side of it. Beneath their house and down the steep slope, overgrown with pine trees and bushes, lay a village huddled closely, surrounded by small farms and caressed by the glittering waters of a river. In the evenings the village seemed as a huge hollow filled with dusk and fantastical forms.

It was nine thirty on a cold night and outside it was still dark. A light drizzle of icy rain was beginning to soak the pine trees and bushes. A damp breeze came in faint gusts with the vague whispering of the cold night. The tall trees faintly rustled wrapped in darkness. Johnson was standing by the window, cradling a glass of brandy in his hand. Then he turned and closed the draperies over the tall windows. He was standing in his imposing study with a heavy mahogany desk, a few chairs and walls to ceiling book cases crammed to bursting with books. The visible parts of the walls were decorated with a few sets of drawings and framed posters.

A short while later he heard Nancy mounting the stairs and walking towards his bedroom. She might be going to set his bed, whose frame and pillars he had reinforced and anchored to the ceiling beams in an artistic way; decorated with the kind of lace and frills over the canopy in hunter green. Suddenly his attention turned to the ringing phone on the desk. He went in a hurry and took the receiver. For a moment he stood there enthralled, eyes agog, at the sweet melodious voice from the phone.

"Mr. Johnson!", A feminine voice erupted in a sweet tenor, "I have no strength to suffer in silence any more! Let me confess that I am damnably attracted. Now it seems to me that you are my everything..I love you!" The voice trailed off in a giggle.

Johnson's heart slammed against his ribcage, despite the female voice was tender, flirting and laughing.

"Really? Tell me who are you?" He asked as his lips curved in an obvious wonder. Then he shrugged his shoulders and scratched his forehead in perplexity. Although Johnson was bewildered at the lady's confession of love, he could feel a sensuous pleasure ran through his whole body, and his nerves tickled. For a moment he was oblivious of his surroundings and surrendered to fantasize a stunning beauty with an adorable face. His mind was filled with a figure of a gorgeous woman in her mid-twenties. Her pretty face framed with wavy, raven-black hair. She had high, full breasts, a flat, firm stomach, jutting ass and long, lean legs.

Johnson stood in a daze, still cradling the receiver.

"Well, young lady, I am so sorry! I am long past all those love affairs and fluers d' amours! I am sorry to confess that I am a married man..."His voice was weak and trembling. Yet it was a resonant baritone that welled up through his broad chest.

"Sir, I am not concerned whether you are married or not..I do not ask you to return my feelings either. I only ask for pity. Please be in the old summer house at ten 'O'clock tomorrow morning. Remember that I am good looking. I know that you are out there in Nilgiri hills, still enjoying the vacation. Then, Why can't you think about something wild happening in your holidays? Can't you even think about unlocking some desires of hidden fantasies?"

A tiny smile tugged at Johnson's lips as the phone line ended abruptly. Placing the receiver back, he blew out a loud breath.

"Absurd! This whole conversation is enticing with sweet friction that aches at some where!"He laughed; then wondered.

"Strange! I love you! When did she find me to fall in love suddenly? Remarkable woman! She's probably too young and romantic if she can fall in love after just a couple of glances. But, who is she? She didn't say her name..."

In his four years of married life Johnson had lost the habit of finer feelings to other women, despite they were beautiful and awesome.

"Of course, I still believe that this phone call is hardly likely to be a joke. It's probably either a college girl or a lady lecturer whom I know; a pretty frivolous and eccentric one. Him! Who could it be?"

Suddenly Johnson remembered that a few weeks ago, while he was taking a stroll around in the college compound, his path had several times crossed that of a young graduate student. She had on a tight, sky blue sleeveless T-shirt that snuggly caressed two of the firmest and largest breasts he had ever seen. Her face and hair were stunning. Long, soft brown curls neatly framed her classic good looks. Her red, moist lips were seemingly soft and sensuous. Her dark eyes were dreamy and her lashes were long. The T-shirt was flimsy enough to allow the sides of her large breasts to spill out through the arm holes. As if mesmerized, Mr. Johnson stared at her and for a briefest moment their eyes locked, leaving him reeling with sexual vertigo!

Once again, in the college library, his personal situation didn't keep him off enjoying the visual pleasure of watching that stunning beauty. It seemed to him that she had somewhat humble job of returning library books to their proper places up on the shelves. One day, a few days after, he was sitting at a table in the canteen, reading a news paper and slowly sipping the tea. When he heard light footsteps, he turned his head and saw her at the entrance door, time and again glancing at him. Then she had walked over to him, took a seat next to him with a broad smile. He remembered that he could only stare.

"Oh, God! Her?"Johnson wondered, "It can't be! Can that girl, an ephemeral creature as far as my mind is concerned, really find it in her to love a married man like me? No, impossible!"

At supper, Mr. Johnson, deep in thought, gazed vacantly at his wife.

"She says she's young and good looking. So, she's surely that graduate student. To tell the truth, in all honesty, I am not even middle aged and ugly looking that no one could ever love me. Well, I am good looking, I must realize. That's why my wife loves me! It's a fact that young ladies love can be pretty blind if they find their lovers are attractive...."

"What are you thinking about?" His wife asked curiously.

"Oh, nothing...I have got a head ache." Johnson lied and looked at his nephew, James. He seemed all groggy as if involuntarily awaken from a deep sleep. Probably, Nancy might have awakened James for inviting him to eat supper. He was fully engrossed in eating the roasted meat, as if gobbling it like a shark. When he began to savour the dessert, Johnson slowly stood upsetting his glass down. Then he took a loud, drawn-out yawn and started towards the wash base. Instead of washing his hands, he began to think again.

"And she probably hopes that I am going to turn up! Won't she be nervous and fidgety when she doesn't find me in that old summer house? Yes, I must go, just out of curiosity!"

That night he fell in to insomnia and his sexual fantasies began to spawn a whole new world of erotic delight. He hoped that his oncoming affair would present endless possibilities in his life and add color and depth to his clandestine desires. It would, anyway, be emotionally satisfying and just a downright fun. Thinking about an extra- marital affair, he was so excited and began to revel in the blush of new found passion.

In the morning, Johnson was as though half asleep, and his small bloated eyes looked out vacantly from under his brows.

"I must go and take a look from the distance. See what's she's like. If she's actually that graduate student, why should I bother about an affair? Especially when the opportunity arises?

Slowly Johnson began to dress. "Where are you getting all dressed up for? It's nearly half past eight…"His wife enquired with a pert, mischievous look. She watched her husband putting on a costly crimson shirt and a fashionable tie.

"No where…I'm just going out for a walk. You know, I have got a bit of head ache and I feel uneasy…"

When he went out, his heart began to beat and seemed to flutter like a bird. Outside everything was fresh, gay and delightful. He could see a long way all round. Shafts of sunlight breaking through the canopy of thick, high branches lit the way and the pungent smell of wild flowers and ferns filled his nostrils. On either side of the glade, there was the silence of woods and the warm moist air overwhelmed him. Finally, as he came in to a gravelly road, he could see the village, and farther down a white church; behind it a eucalyptus wood stretched far and wide down the hill. The breeze that ushered in the dawn had freshened and mists were still whirling in the ravines. There was a perfect flood of light everywhere. As he went along, he saw the people from the small cottages, moving about against the bright green background of foliage suffused with the light of the morning sun. Shyly watching the faces of women in the newer by tea estate, he entered a long avenue that led to the old summer house.

"Him! If it's that frivolous graduate student, then she's probably sitting in the summer house. Now it's past ten…"He thought nervously as he saw the old summerhouse through the young greeneries of tall trees. He trudged towards it swiftly. A lust that seemed handed down from his weird fantasy was still boiling in his blood, raising his excitement. He made haste to get the summerhouse through the green track on the high grass and bushes tangled by the creepers.

"Well, first of all, I will just have a look from the distance, "he thought as he moved through the tangled bushes, "what am I afraid of? What a timid fool I am! Don't be afraid of and shy you,young married man!"But, Johnson's heart began to beat even louder.

Against his will, he suddenly imagined himself standing in the dim light of the summer house. In his imagination,he glimpsed the young graduate student dressed up in a provocation red spandex miniskirt with a red knit top and a pair of matching high heels that accentuated her well-developed legs. He could barely keep his eyes off her. She seemed as if ashamed of her love and trembling slightly as she approached him. Despite of her shyness,she was smiling at him with her soft, sensuous lips. As she drew nearer, he embraced her and slowly kissed. Then she slowly moved him behind and nailed him against the wall with her body, pushing her large breasts in to his chest and trapping his manhood in the cleft between her legs. He could feel her hot tongue probing his entire mouth. As she moaned, he began to undress her, still ravenously kissing and caressing the entire length of her sexy body.

Suddenly Mr. Johnson's right leg hit hard on a small boulder.

"Oh!" He cried with pain, "If I weren't married, it wouldn't be so bad.."Now he thought remorsefully, trying to drive the sinful thoughts out of his mind. Then he heaved a sigh.

"But….once in a life time it wouldn't do any harm to try it. Otherwise I might reach my death-bed without knowing what it's like! My God! Four years, it has been really an unblemished service to my wife. Why don't I think that's enough for her? Yes, that's enough for her!"

Trembling from head to foot and holding his breath, Johnson approached the old,dilapidated summer house draped in ivy and wild creepers with broad leaves. He could smell the dampness and the mould.

"There seems to be no one. 'He said as he looked inside. Then he slowly went in. But he was astonished to see a human figure sitting in a corner. It was a man's figure. With a rumbling growl, Johnson looked more closely and recognized his nephew. A fresh breeze ran over his face. Johnson wrapped himself more closely in to his cloak and tried hard to repress his involuntary emotion. It was rather the kind of a feeling of revulsion.

"Oh, James! it's you!", He mumbled, not hiding his displeasure as he took off his cap and sat down next to him on the cement bench.

"Oh, uncle! it's me! What a surprise!" Answered James in a quivering, albeit annoyed voice. Johnson could watch his eyes flashing and apparently,for him, his nephew seemed crazed, frenzied and he could also sense so much hatred in the fire burning in his eyes. A minute, or perhaps two went by in silence.

"Excuse me, uncle, "Finally, James began with a wild stare at Mr. Johnson, "But I would politely ask you to leave me alone. I am thinking about my on-site research…and, I am sorry to say that, any ones presence, even yours disturbs me…"

As if irritated and with a sudden oblique glance at his nephew, Mr. Johnson remarked furiously.

"Oh, in that case you should find yourself an even darker place, I must say, an avenue somewhere outside. It's easier to think and recollect in the fresh air…"Mr. Johnson suddenly stopped short as he saw his nephew fisted his hands, gesticulating and flashing his eyes. As if wondered at his strange demeanor, Mr. Johnson ripped his eyes from James and began to speak in clenched teeth.

"James..listen..I..that is..I want to have a nap on this cement bench.."

James listened dumbly as if he did not understand Mr. Johnson's language.

"Holy crap! You want to have a nap, and I want to think seriously out of my on-site research!"He growled. "But, any way, my research is more important. You please take leave at once…"

"What shall I say to this incorrigible scamp!"Mr. Johnson wondered. He leaned against the edge of the cement bench and grew pensive. His pale face was distorted and perfectly still, as if he was trying not to listen his nephew.

"What a horrid situation!"He murmured to himself,trying to maintain a casual air.

Again there was perfect silence. By the time, Mr. Johnson, who had given free rein to his imagination and every moment fancied he heard the sound of approaching footsteps of his graduate student, suddenly stood up and pleaded in a lugubrious voice.

"Look! I beg you, James! You are younger than me and my nephew. You should at least have little respect to me. You know, I am ill and tired. And I want to sleep on this bench for a while. Please go away!"

"Oh, uncle, it's disgusting! What the devil for should I go out there? No. I would better sit here for a while. I won't go way, on principle!"

"That's egotistic! That's pure arrogance, James!..And I beg you! Just once in my life, I beg you..please go out!" James shook his head, snarled and his face started twitching. His look of smugness and exquisite refinement a short while ago had vanished.

"No!" he shouted. Mr. Johnson could discern a repulsive expression of hatred on his face.

"What a swine! 'he thought to himself, "So, he won't let me see her. There will be no rendezvous, of course, while he's here. There can't be…"

"Look James" he said calmly, "I am asking you for the last time. Show me what an obedient, intelligent and young educated man you are.."

"Him, I don't know why you keep pestering me."James answered, shrugging his shoulders, "And I say, I won't go…."

At the very moment a woman's silhouette, a stunning figure, appeared at the entry of the summer house. She was attired in a thick cable-knit sweater and dark jeans, wrapped in a long over coat. A small cap was perched on her head and her elegant face was partially hidden with oversized sunglasses. Her long brown hairs were dancing in the breeze. Suddenly she stopped and glanced in to the summer house.

Mr. Johnson and James looked at her in wonder. When she parted her red, moist lips as if in astonishment, a single monarch butterfly had somehow gotten near her face. It fluttered around her face and slowly swirled back on the warm breeze toward the thick foliage of creepers. She paused for a few seconds in confusion. Seeing Mr. Johnson and James together, her face frowned and suddenly she disappeared.

Mr. Johnson could still hear the loud clump of her sturdy boots down the steps. He realized that the flare of anticipation and clandestine desire died within her, the moment she saw him with James. R. Johnson swallowed and suddenly his face darkened.

"Oh, my God! She's gone!"He ground out words between nearly clenched teeth, unconsciously jerking his head toward James. James met his flaring eyes. He was pissed!

"Oh, She saw this scoundrel and she's gone! All is lost!" Mr. Johnson mumbled. He waited a few minutes, put on his cap, and said disgustedly.

"James you are a swine and scoundrel! You are mean and stupid! I am never going to speak to you again…."

"Oh, I am glad to hear it. "growled James. He stood up and put on his slippers.

"Uncle, I will never forget you that your presence just now has done me a wrong which I won't forgive you!" The last words he uttered were in tears that would move a stone!

Mr. Johnson left the summer house and strode quickly toward the town.

"It was an opportunity that comes once in a life time "He seethed. "And that swine got in unexpectedly and interfered. Now she's insulted!"

While walking, he took the slim cell phone out of the pocket of his pants and saw the message screen popped up on. He read the message in a hurry. The sultry Goddess he saw a few minutes ago as if a vision from heaven, had texted the following.

"Sir, I had planned to share the occasion only with you. When I went happily, I had no idea what was in store for me. And what was out there? I felt a lump in my heart! Are you unashamedly awaiting me out there for threesome? I am mortally offended! Good bye forever, you philistine!"

A quivering sigh came through Mr. Johnson's lips. His head was filled with a heavy fog, and through the haze in his head, he heard her sarcasm sounded with unusual frequency. His mouth felt dry and sticky.

"Oh, James, you swine! All is lost! A chance like that might never easily come again!"

He was overwhelmed with a feeling of remorse and frustration and he even wanted to cry. With a pallid face and sweat broke out on his face, Mr. Johnson shuffled his way towards the town so as to reach out a bar.

When Mr. Johnson had left him alone, James took off his glasses, wiped them and recalled the event took place in the summer house. Although he felt sorry for his uncle, he was thinking about the appearance of the woman. He felt that he could find no respite from his great annoyance which prevented him fully enjoying the visual pleasure. He found her body set a standard by which all other females could be judged. She's probably the anonymous woman who sent him the mail yesterday, inviting him at the summer house. James was near panic as he realized that he might never see her again. He didn't want to lose her. The woman of such dazzling, extraordinary beauty. Then he immediately realized that it wasn't Sophia whom he had expected to meet in the summer house. He came down slowly and regained his composure, hoping that if he would search the row of big houses along the road and restaurants in the nearby town, he could find her fascinating figure.

James made up his mind, hurried through the ramshackle summerhouse and walked through the front door. Then he went down the rickety steps. Finally he came before the motor bike parked down the avenue. He heaved a sigh and drove down the lane that silhouetted the buildings in shades, despite the blistering sun made a head ache.

Mr. Johnson came after late that evening. He was excessively drunk and tipsy, and also at the very height of his nervous crisis. When he reached the end of the long yard, the front door creaked open and his wife greeted him graciously.

"Johnson, dear! 'she said with a broad smile, "If I start saying something not quite so to you, please don't get bothered…and be amiable as you were ever with me.."

Nancy giggled, huddling in her cashmere shawl.

Mr. Johnson shrugged as if he couldn't understand her, and yet his back seemed to have shrunk from grief. He didn't reply to her. As he walked in front of her, he looked wondered at the exquisitely decorated drawing room. Everything right there seemed completely rearranged. The litters in the corners were swept and dusted off. The Italian marble floor was shining after neatly scrubbed and the walls were brushed off and clean. It seemed to him that Nancy had deliberately made crucial changes in his house.

"What do you think?"Nancy asked as she seized him by the arm and led him around the wood-paneled room that simply, but beautifully furnished with couches and crisp linen.

"Ah, it's cute!"Johnson sounded enthusiastic as he went to see a succession of brightly lit rooms.

Meanwhile, the crimson streak behind the house and the hillock had faded away. Slowly, it had grown darker and the objects had lost their contours.

At supper Mr. Johnson and James stared at their plates in gloomy silence. It seemed each one of them hated the other with all his heart.

"Well, we are going to have an excellent supper; in the modern style. I am going to serve it.."Nancy said as she laid salted, marinated and all other kinds of delicacies on the table. There were also dishes of boiled rice, roasted chicken, Tuna fish and much else.

While Mr. Johnson and James were expecting to be served, Nancy suddenly burst out laughing.

"What are you laughing about? Mr. Johnson barked at his wife, "Only idiots laugh with out reason!" Nancy's mocking laugh had irritated the hell out of him.

Nancy stopped laughing and glared at Johnson for a moment.

"I am sorry, dear. But you must tell me who was the lady who called you yesterday…"

Johnson watched all the mischief in Nancy's eyes and wondered.

"Me? No..no..I got no phone call at all.." Mr. Johnson replied in confusion. "it's your imagination."

"Go on, pull the other one! Blatant lies! Congenital liar! My dear, why don't you admit that you got a lady's phone call? Are you afraid of me to admit?"

Mr. Johnson turned bright red and leant over his plate. "Well, I know all about the phone call! Because I was the one who called you, using the maid's cell phone! Honestly! Ha..ha!" Then Nancy turned to James.

"And you, James! Tell me honestly something about the mail you received!" Nancy was giggling as if in a frenzy.

"How can you talk about it aloud, teasing each one of us!" James thought in anguish. He raised his head, made the sign of the cross and murmured.

"Oh, Lord, I wish I could leave here at once!" He felt unbearably ashamed that he was amazed to find human shame could be so acute and overpowering.

Nancy stopped laughing and began to serve, humming a melodious tune. When she reached to James, he felt even more ashamed that he tried to smile. Nancy patted on his back, understanding how ashamed were both of them, as if being treated like silly brats.

"Nancy, what stupid joke is this? But the woman who came out over there? who is she?"

Jhonson growled as if he couldn't understand the strange occurrence at there.

"See for yourself!" Nancy giggled again as she made a step toward the stand in the corner. She stared rapturously at his face and picked up the phone.

"Hello? Can you get down fast here? come to the dining room. Supper is ready…"

Five minutes later, hastily dressed, a woman around twenty-five appeared in the doorway.

"Look James!"said Johnson thoroughly appalled, nudging at James's elbow and running his eyes up and down at the woman. His mouth and eyes were wide open and he was absolutely paralyzed in shock. If he was lying at somewhere in that state, he might have seemed as if a motionless corpse just brought up from the morgue cellar for dissection!

Jhonson's wide eyes crawled over her body like lice. She was wearing a form-fitting vintage suit that did full justice to her voluptuous figure.Her cream silk blouse revealed the merest hint of lace detailing on her bra. The cream colour blouse emphasized the wavy, brown highlights in her tousled hair. Her eyes seemed enormous and her cheeks were slightly flushed. Her slender, but soft body in the tight dress enhanced every curve, including the smallness of her waist.

Johnson rubbed his eyes with his left hand and tried to smile at her.

"Ah, it's a pleasure to meet you! Please take your seat..."He mumbled, stretching out his hand and assuming an inviting expression.

Meanwhile, James was also staring at the woman in wonder. His eyes seemed dazzled, his breath caught, and he could feel an incomprehensible sensation running down the length of his body.

"Oh, thank you, sir. Your house looks awesome!"The young lady remarked as she slipped in to a chair opposite Johnson..

Mr. Johnson grinned widely and waved down to his wife. Nancy went up to them and introduced the young lady to her husband.

"Darling, see, this is Rachel, one of my colleagues. She has decided to spent the vacation with us. Nice, isn't it?"

"Oh, is it true, Rachel? Glad to meet you..."Johnson said in a quivering voice, frought with feeling, and there was something childishly faint hearted in his continuing words.

Rachel smiled elegantly, but soon it slipped when she saw that Mr. Johnson was more tense and upset.

"Mr. Johnson you look so sad and tense.."Rachel said, smiling again.

Then Nancy sat next to Johnson and intervened."Rachel, dear! He never get restless often. But, unfortunately, today something unhappy afforded him a certain discomfort..."

Nancy sipped a glass of water, and continued."You know, a gorgeous woman flashed by the window of an old summer house, like a shooting star, might be the reason for this melancholy..."

"Nancy,this is terrible!"Mr. Johnson frowned, fidgeting in his chair. He felt so angry and upset.

"Oh, don't get angry, you turkey cock!" Nancy giggled as if she was interested to hurt her husband's vanity.

Mr. Johnson listened dumbly, said no more and fully engrossed in eating.

Nancy stroked his curly hair with affection and said."Poor hubby! But what else could I do? Listen, Rachel. We had to wash the floors today. And,think, how was I to get these lazy fellows out of the house? It was the only way! And thank you Rachel for your part to make an unforgettable scene for my Turkey cocks!"

James was listening Nancy. He smiled at her with a surge of admiration, and ceased to look on his uncle with such loathing. But, obviously to provoke him, he passed a glass of water to Mr. Johnson who kept silent. James murmured as Mr. Johnson drank up at a draught.

"You sex freak, drink up your fill!"Then he blew a flying kiss to Rachel and burst out laughing.

CHAPTER 2

AN EROTIC DREAMER KNOCKED OFF!

After supper Johnson walked in to the bed room and threw himself down on the bed, fully clothed, staring up at the ceiling. The cold night felt as if it were so many years old, even though he knew it was only a little past Ten o'clock. He was drunken, tired and yet he was not completely boozed, but depressed. He felt a faint bitter taste of intangible defeat stirring with in him. An opportunity lost forever. Or rather an opportunity created to laugh at him! The first faint dawn of his secret ambitions, dreams of sexual fantasy baffled with a mixture of emotions brought out an intangible defeat still within him.

"What shall I do?I am aroused! Am I destined to reach my throbbing, drooling cock and cry! What has been shattered in my mind is an exquisite feeling of passion; to explore dreams that so many of them view as forbidden to a married man. I hoped for a secret rendezvous, a passionate coupling with a gorgeous woman that would leave me delighted and etched deep in my memory forever."

His wandering thoughts went their own course. Then he heard footsteps and the doors closed. Nancy smiled at him revealing a row of her captivating teeth. As she advanced, she saw him so tired and exhausted that its weary lines etched deeply in to his cheeks.

"Are you alright, dear? I hope I haven't purposely insulted you "Nancy smiled suddenly. He looked askance at her. When she smiled, her face took on a strange, bright beauty, he thought. Nancy stood by the bed, looking intently at his face.

"Darling, I am sorry. I think I behaved coarsely. You might think that I have forgotten my manners. Forgive me.."She said awkwardly. Johnson smiled back.

"Oh, Nancy I am not bothered. It's all right. I am well and happy. What did you downstairs was very little.."

Nancy's eyes searched him for a moment. "I am glad to see you aren't offended.."

Nancy said as she stripped her night gown over her head. When she turned, she could see his eyes focused on her breasts and then his gaze wandered lower. She smiled and dropped to her knees on the bed. When Johnson half raised himself, she pressed her face lovingly against him.

"Darling, please leave those new found passion and fascination. It's all undesirable in conjugal life. You know, fantasies can spawn only myriad colors of erotic delight. Let me admit that, it's blissfully sensual and alluringly exotic. But never try to reap the benefits of clandestine desires. Let it only be weird fantasies, if you are boring. If you ever try to enact it, it's really immoral and basically sinful......"Nancy crooned, raising her head and looking over his face. Then her wandering eyes traced down his body covered in bed sheet. It seemed to Johnson that her eyes popped up. Licking her sensuous lips she whispered with a little cry.

"Jeez, look! I can see a pup tent beneath the sheet!"

"Nancy, you can lift that sheet off! I want to revel tonight!"Johnson blurted out huskily. Then he said aside too! As if an eager erotic lover thrilled to explore!

"*Yes, I want to revel in the blush of my new found passion and fantasy!. oh,Rachel!*"

Johnson slid off his sweater and pants in a second on the floor and sucked in breath as Nancy began to tingle all over his face with hot kisses. Slowly, the couple melded and flew in to each other. Suddenly an icy rain lashed down outside. And they were illumined for a fraction of a second by a white glow through the window. It was followed by a thunder-clap.

Half an hour later, after relaxing for a few minutes, Nancy wriggled around in Johnson's embrace and looked at his face. He could tell from the light in her eyes that she was satisfied and she wanted to say and share something to him.

"Would you like Rachel?"She asked in a voice that sounded innocent enough.

"Why ask me? I don't know." Johnson lied.

"Rachel is from Kottayam.She's appointed here a few weeks ago. And now she had to leave the rented cottage. She want to stay here temporarily until she find a new apartment. Will you permit her to stay here?"

"Sure enough"Johnson lifted one eye brow and tossed her his trade mark wolfish grin.

"Oh,but I am rather afraid of you."Nancy said ruefully, rubbing his shoulder tentatively as if she were unsure about his ill manners and disposition.

"Darling, don't worry. It's nothing. I am not that type of a Casanova!"

Johnson laughed, hauling Nancy against him and delivering a kiss on her delicious lips. She tasted like wild honey and sex so he deepened the kiss. When he finally lifted his head, they were both breathing heavily.

"Dear, I trust you."Nancy said as her eyes caught his and held his gaze. He could see her eyes searching for the right words from him.

"You can always trust me."Johnson caught her hand and brought it to his lips.

"Thank you, Johnson."Nancy smiled and stretched herself toward the desk by the bed. Then she took hold of a book with her hand and sat half raised on the bed. Resting her head on the pillow lay over the head board, and reclining, she began to leaf through the pages.

Then she remembered her days at St. Lawrence High school. So many guileless baby blues, that feigned innocence and slim shoulders that shrugged demurely beneath their cheer leading uniforms in the class rooms. Often she arched one brow, crossed her arms and pierced each student with that dreaded mistress stare. How incorrigible they are!

With a roll of her eyes, a student might be closing a magazine in the class room. Another shuffled papers round, trying desperately to look busy with learning. And at the rear, she heard someone sniggered, followed by bleats of laughter. Enraged, she would stroll to the back bench and scream, leveling her gaze at them.

"Excuse me, block heads! You must hold it down or I will put in a call to each one of your parents this time.."

She could see them freeze and the room fell silent as those all guilty raised their eyes in terror at her!

That's an school mistress life-from watch to watch, from lesson to lesson, always on alert to guide them for a better future.

A blush of pride suffused Nancy's face; and slowly she switched on the table lamp. When Nancy began to read half way through, Johnson glanced at her idly with his sleepy, sour eyes. He felt a heaviness and debility in all his limbs. Exhausted and bathed in sweat, Johnson heaved a sigh and drifted in to a profound sleep.

After half an hour reading Nancy fell in to a state of weary drowsiness which passed in to sleep.

And the whole nature was also fast asleep; the deep, unbroken sleep that comes before mid night. Outside, the moonlit night seemed magnificent than ever. Everything was perfectly still, and many of the stars, that only appeared after the rain a short while ago, had been high up in the sky. The waves of frozen mist were rolling down and spreading over the plains. The sky was soon left with a full moon, sprinkled with stardust.

Although Mr. Johnson was fast asleep, he rolled over his back, with his left arm wrapped around Nancy's waist. From the glass window ran a beam of blurred whiteness of the moon light to his bed.

It seemed that his sleeping mind was fighting off unwanted memories that surfaced. Soon his sweaty face was suffused with an innocently, child liker smile; for he was beginning to weave a sweet dream!

Let's recount his dream!

He was riding a motor bike on the winding road, stomping on the accelerator, with his eyes bulging in his goggles, like a bear! Soon he passed stoplight controlling traffic over a narrow covered bridge and sped fast away with all those pine trees shielded the view of the road. He was driving down early that morning to visit some of his friends near love dale, a beautiful old colonial town in Ootty, and some twenty miles away. The sentinel row of tall pine trees and thick foliage either side of the road were glowing in a final blaze of glory before the snow of winter fall.

Johnson suddenly pulled over when he saw an attractive woman wearing jeans, flannel shirt and sturdy hiking boots down the road. She was climbing up a muddy trail that meandered above the lake shore. It was a campsite of tourists. As he watched he could see some of them hauling a canoe to the lake. The blue ripples whisk along the lake was lifting rhythmically the canoe. In the distance, half hidden by the trees, round, low hills were seen in broad undulations.

When she saw Johnson, she held her head high and smiled. She walked toward his direction. Then she stopped and stretched out a hand for help, as if she wanted to climb up from the bottom.

She was a tall, graceful lady with regular, attractive features and dark blue eyes. Her lashes were dark and long.

"You please stay there. I am coming.." Johnson said as he went over to help her. He offered her his hand with a smile. With one powerful pull she was all the way up.

"Thank you." She smiled elegantly. Johnson watched her closely. Her face was beautiful. Her lips were soft and sensuous. The fullness of her mouth enticed him further.

Johnson felt the fragrance of the morning damp gave way to the penetrating odor of perfume and sweat.

"Hello, Johnson. I am glad it's you!"She bestowed a sugary smile. Johnson beamed with pleasure.

"Oh, Rachel! I have never known that you were an enthusiastic hiker!"

"Oh, I love to hike. It's just like having fun.."

"Really?" Johnson's eyes lit up, "To run marathons in chilly weather?"He laughed.

"Well, let's go round the lake for a walk. You know, there's a nice spot to rest.A silent place. What do you say?" He asked as he parked his bike under a tree; a shady recess down the road.

"That sounds good.."Rachel said in a throaty whisper and nodded.

Johnson's eyes warmed as she neared. He remained standing, a silent smile on his face. His brown eyes were fastened on her tits.

"Christ! I am driving crazy with her presence!" He thought as she moved even closer to him.

There was a perfect flood of light with the glow of dawn spreading. As the they walked down, the streaks of gold stretched across the sky. They made their way down the bottom of a slope, through the thin vapory mist, where a small tree spread out its palmated branches over the water. As Rachel leaned closer and continued talking, Johnson put his arm around her shoulders, his finger tips idly brushing the top of her tit. With the other hand, Johnson pointed toward a dense clump of bushes near the lake.

"Rachel, dear. That place is a best look out spot in all of this area..."

"Oh, really." She smiled coyly and leaned even more closely against him. Her smiling face was a few inches away from his. He felt her warm breath on his cheek and smelled the fragrance of her hair as it brushed against his face. He could see a bright light came in to her eyes.

"Surprise! Is something bothering you, Johnson?"She asked, narrowing her eyes.

Johnson shook his head with a puzzled look. There was laughter still in her eyes as she watched his face.

"You look nervous. Any trouble?"

"Oh, am I just a deuce!"He wondered. Then he blurted out quickly.

"Oh, Rachel, dear! I am...I am..just thinking how to flirt with you, begging for more attention!"

Rachel could see his eyes wandering over her. He was staring at her flannel shirt, that snuggly caressed two of the firmest and largest breasts he had ever seen!

Rachel turned round with a wheezy snicker and gasped.

"Then..okay.. you can flirt with me.. But it's better when you have someone to share your feelings. You don't stick things in to yourself. But.. But.. I think it's better to share your feelings with Nancy." Rachel blurted out and gasped again.

Johnson was listening hopefully. But his curiosity was piqued at her last words.

Rachel walked in front of him in silence. Johnson was sad for a moment. Yet he could have a sneak preview of her enormous ass in her tight jeans.

The melancholy, monotonous chirping of the crickets and the distant call of a quail disrupted the silence. Johnson followed her, trying to ward off the torment, and waiting to snatch a few hours at the lake side with Rachel.

Through the slender tree trunks, the rays of the sun, just raised, beat on his back. He got a good stretch, drank in the damp, fragrant air and continued walking.

They descended the steep lake bank together and, finally, sat down on a wooden bench. The seat was near the water's edge, between dense clumps of young bushes. It was really a wonderful spot, hidden from the rest of the world, providing total privacy for enjoying the view of nature. The right side of the bench was surrounded by a high fence and trees.

Some scattered black clouds scudded low over the lake out of the North West. By now, the purple sun was floating upwards with streaks of crimson across the sky. It shed no warmth, but shone more brightly. The trees, covered with frost in the morning, looked now all golden and stood out picturesquely against the azure sky.

A fresh wind softly stirred up and drove before them the fallen, crumpled leaves..Far from them, over the lake, flew merlins and orioles, the migrating birds, with shrill cry. There were low waves, with small white crest, covered the whole of the lake's vast, blue surface.

The cold, damp wind pierced them to the marrow of their bones. In the passing wind, the sodden trees, their branches lowered down, scattered big drops against them. Distantly, on the left side and along the campsite, a rider struck his horse on the muzzle with his left hand, and galloped off at a break neck pace.

Rachel peered up at him. He was as handsome as she imagined in her mind about the man. The man she dreamed about often, carved and molded in masculine beauty.

"Johnson, do you really attracted to me?" She crooned softly in to his ear.

"Of course, I do. I wouldn't miss a chance of being with you all day for the world."He told her with unaccustomed pride.

Rachel gave him a beguiling smile "But, Johnson, you are a married man. And Nancy is not only my colleauge, but my dear friend. She's very dear to me. I don't want to spoil your life either. I can't accept your love. It would be as jumpy as a grass hoper in fire…"Rachel said with a feeling of deepening fear and slowly she moved a little way off from him.

Johnson's heart was pounding quite so hard. She didn't say that she loved him. But she showed her concern that she knew everything and she'd a feeling for him. The only thing she wanted to prove is that she hadn't come to destroy his family.

Rachel smiled and reached out a hand to him, "Want some advice?"She asked.

He looked at her doubtfully. "Oh, my good lady, no more advice!"He replied bluntly. Johnson could see anguish seeped in to her, building her own apprehension, her own fears. But she knew Johnson cared about her like a companion, and maybe he loved her. But how can she accept his love, still staying at his house. She took his hand and nibbled on it in confusion.

"Rachel, I have tried to forget you. But I can't, darling. For you look so damn good and your presence feel so damn good. I am helpless!"His words trailed off.

Rachel looked in to his eyes that flamed with passion. She knew they mirrored her own.

"Johnson," she mumbled, "I think, I think you are attracted to me for one simple reason. You just want a unique thrill of a casual encounter..Just sex.. and..of course not love.."

A small canoe with two tourists sitting astride, sailed on the lake, cutting through the cold surface of the lake, dappled in sparkling ripples. While one of them paddled along, the other looked rather comical, balancing a bottle of whisky on his forehead.

Johnson looked at the canoe, then at the hedge of trees basking in the early sun that seemed to be engraved on the sky. A conical mountain was silently towering above the trees. The lake below was turquoise, vast as the sky overturned.

"Rachel, so, you means that only? Sex!"

"Exactly!"Rachel snorted, a slight smile tugged at her curved lips.

Johnson slapped a hand to his forehead. "Don't tell me that, Rachel. This is not about sex. It's something ethereal. It's really about love..."

"Love!" Rachel cocked a brow in surprise. "You love me! But, I don't love you. I don't even know you yet, Johnson. All I know is that you are a family man, an excellent professor at the college...."

"You are a nut.."Johnson murmured. Rachel propped her hands on her hips and stared at Johnson as if she couldn't understand him.

"Why is everything about love with you? Do you think that you can date with any woman you love with your butt load of money?."She asked.

Johnson tossed Rachel his own look of disgust. An awkward pause hung over them for a moment before Johnson cleared his throat.

"Hey, Rachel, I have never seen such a sweet woman get so mad. My lady, you rather look like a wet hen, all ruffled up and ready to peck my eyes out!" Johnson laughed aloud and it sounded like pieces of metal rubbing together. "But, I love you Rachel, with all the heart. You are so lovely!"

Rachel leaned back on the bench and burst out laughing. And before she could stop, Johnson pulled her tighter to him and lowered his head. He kissed her sweet, wet lips ravenously. He felt she tasted of all things good. All things sexy and right!

Rachel was not expected to his sudden advance to her. She gave a moan of surrender and angled her head so he could deepen his kiss. Slowly her arms curled around his neck, pulling him to her. Then he went on eagerly, his heaving chest pressing against the delicious softness of her breasts.

"Mmm.." She groaned, rocking her hips against the erection straining his pants.

"Mmmm, Johnson!" Rachel panted, running her nails down his back and forcefully trying to disengage from his embrace. Johnson's hold was tight and he moved his head hungrily to her breast. Suddenly, she forcefully pushed his head off from her breast.

"No!" She cried and got in her feet. Then she peered down at him, framed against the sun. She was suddenly feeling guilty. She couldn't rejoice in the feel of him.

"Please, Johnson.." She mumbled, fighting off the sheer lust raging inside her.

"Please, what?" What do you want Rachel?" He growled. His look, so teasing before, didn't seem playful now.

"Please not now, meet me later." Rachel crooned with hesitation rearing its head inside her.

Johnson swallowed hard with evident disappointment. "Okay. But you don't say much later."

"No." Rachel said with a shy smile, her fingers idly dipping in to the waist of her jeans. But she was thinking as if to say something to him.

Jonson you forget your wife. You are infidel and shallow. You are so vile. You are not worthy of the black lace thong I wore..."

Rachel looked at him, still smiling and saying nothing. For some time Johnson stared adoringly at her beautiful face. It was awesome, with ebony curls around her face.

Then it really seemed to him that his sensitive soul had been able to read a message in her glance. He believed that she had forgiven him and accepted his overtures.

"One day, all of her reservations would be flying as I took her in. And it won't be much later!" Johnson thought. He would touch every inch of her luscious body and marvel at the rise of her breasts, at her smooth planes and deep, sensitive hollows! He would dot small, wet kisses on her face, on her neck and down the edge of her breasts with dedicated attention. "Yes, yes!" He felt insane by the desire to have Rachel one day. And it won't be much later!

Rachel seemed to sense his frustration and his need. "Johnson, my bad boy, please get up. Let's go.."

Finally she spoke, darting a quick look round.

"Yeah," Johnson sighed heavily and got on his feet. As he walked along with her, his heart hammered heavily in his constricted chest.

They climbed up and walked toward a pasture ground hidden from the view by the heavy wall of trees that surrounded the ground. A little later they heard the lowing of the cows. In the bushes, so many birds had broken in to a loud song. Up above, the red flushed sky had turned blue. They looked at the herd of cows grazing peacefully on the ground.

"Johnson, I am so excited today. Look around here. The cows grazing, the birds flying in flocks with a concert of music, and the warm sun light! It seems that only it's here on this earth, there's a clean, graceful poetic life...."

Down the pasture ground appeared a man riding a small light-bay horse with black mane and short tail. Then, all of a sudden, the rider slipped toward the trees and disappeared behind the foliage.

As they crossed the pasture ground, they could see a piebald cow stood in a swampy, narrow stream up to its knees and lazily swung its wet tail from time to time. Farther down, in the slimy water, ducks were busily splashing and waddling about. On the low bank, a bovine young ling with a small tail and short ruffled mane was running on its unsteady legs after its mother. Its shrill whinnying reached to them.

Rachel stopped, and squealed with pleasure like a teenage girl. Then he could see her jump up and down excitedly. He laughed. Then his naughty eyes hovered over her jiggling ass. A surge of lust, entirely unexpected, skittered through his body.

"All right. I must wait. It won't be much later!" Johnson said to himself, flushed with excitement.

A breath of morning freshness came from the pine wood. The morning sun rose higher, playing on the golden cross of a church on the hill, visible in the far distance.

They walked swiftly and entered on the fringe of the pine wood.

"Johnson, let's go through that way."Rachel whispered, seizing by the arm and leading him toward the glade. They continued walking; winding their way along a seemingly endless trail with huge columns of pine trees either side of them.

"How much longer?" Johnson asked anxiously, his eyes shifting from the way to her radiant face.

"A few minutes.."Rachel smiled. "Now take a left turn.."She swerved on to a dirt road, coasted half mile down a gravel-strewn hill. Finally they arrived at a country road that ended to rest in front of a magnificent house, highly ornate and brightly painted. The road closed on itself at that point, forming a circular drive way.

"We are here." She announced. "Look, my car is parked out there."She said, pointing to a car parked by a black wrought-iron gate.

"Johnson, please get in. I will drop you there on the highway, where you had parked the bike..."

Johnson smiled and made a grab for her. Then he forcefully pressed his lips to her. Before his hand reached to palm her ass, Rachel pushed him off with a giggle.

"You naughty! You have to wait. Only later!"She crooned as she savored the taste of his kiss.

"Okay..Okay. Rachel, you know my answer. Not much later!"Johnson growled as he got in the front seat with her. Rachel took the wheel and started the car as Johnson felt a stab of frustrated desire go through him.

"Hm,I think this is going to be a pretty dull run..."He said looking out the grit road. He was right. Rachel's driving became bumpy for some minutes until she drove in to the main road. Every so often they came up on a series of small cottages where they could see villagers moving aimlessly about. While driving, Rachel asked a stream of questions about the villagers and the hill station which he answered interestingly. The path gradually ran an uphill.. Down the right side of the road and half mile round, lay a vast tea estate that sparkled picturesquely against the azure sky. The hoar frost was still white at the bottom of the hollows.

As they journeyed through the outskirts to a winding road, where a few kilometers away he had parked the motorbike, Johnson felt his heart heavy. He had to leave her at there.

"Rachel, I enjoyed so far with you. I hope that I can drop my place this evening and have few beers together..." He said with a smile as his face wandered down from her face to her sheer flannel top with no bra, highlighting her outstanding boobs and large nipples.

"Thank you, Johnson. I am happy to be invited. I appreciate your hospitality and zest for living. I will certainly wait there with Nancy..." she said as if tentatively agreed to his suggestion.

Johnson stared at her, speechless for a moment, as sudden anger ran through him in cold waves.

"Damn you. I just wanted to be with you to share my feelings. It's not an invitation to drink together with my wife's presence..Do you think that I want to flirt with you or going to tell you a really wild and sexy tale?.."Johnson snorted in an unsteady voice, fraught with emotion.

Rachel turned her face and studied his face for a moment. She saw a slight hint of moisture in his eyes. She tried to smile, although she sensed a shrinking in her as she met a piercing look from his eyes. She shifted the stick, allowing the car to surge forward and hug the curves of the road she was familiarized. Then she passed a turn and suddenly pulled over in to a large rest stop near the lake.

"Hell, am I going to be a perpetual tragic figure in his family quarrel.."Rachel thought for a moment. She lifted her shoulder in a feeble shrug and said.

"Okay, Johnson, I will wait for you alone." Rachel moved forward to him with a grinning face, tilted her head slightly and pressed her lips on his cheek.. Then she gave him a crushing hug, before he got out. She said good bye and closed the door.

Johnson laughed low and tromped toward his motor bike. He started his bike and raced along, watching for a moment at her car in the rear view mirror as she took a turn back. He felt as happy as a soaring lark with hot desires churning in his breast. His mind, as happy as ever, was equipped with a huge palette that could add color to his loving relationship with Rachel

When the doorbell rang that evening, Rachel was as nervous as if it were her first date, though she knew nothing to worry about. She went downstairs and opened the door. Her nervousness was dissolved with an impish wink Johnson threw as he went in the hall. He had brought her beers and pancake

"Hello, Johnson. You are up early!" She exclaimed. Her hair was all messed up with a mass of taffy brown curls. Her cheeks flushed and her eyes glow.

Johnson smiled, curled his right arm around her, his fingertips dipping in to her waist and slowly stroking her hip.

"Where's Nancy?"He enquired anxiously. His voice echoed shrilly through the hall. He looked on a clock over one of the desks. It was past four thirty.

"She went for shopping a short while ago. You got my beers ready?" Rachel asked as she moved away from him and tying a blue terry-cloth robe around her. From the glimpse, Johnson caught her shapely thighs beneath the robe as she moved. He guessed she was wearing nothing underneath.

Johnson smiled and followed her silently up the staircase and in to a room. The room was neatly furnished with cushioned chairs and a round table. A large red rug was spread over most of the floor. There was a huge led screen at the far end of the room.

"Johnson, I think you helped yourself to drink from the bar."Rachel whispered, looking at his drunk-sodden face and red, inflamed eyes. She could smell the stale reek of alcohol on his breath

"Oh, we had a party together.." Johnson said as he burped and he picked up two bottles of beer out of a plastic bag.

"Old pals. Very bad guys!" He began, sitting at the round table and wiping away the perspiration with his left hand. Then he put the beer bottles on the table.

"Sit down, and have a drink." He said, opening a beer bottle and pushing it toward her.

"Okay!" she smiled with a funny light in her eyes.

"You like pan cakes?"He asked as he opened the other bottle.

"Yeah, I am in the mood for pancakes." Rachel nodded as she slid on to a cushioned chair opposite him.

Johnson picked up a packet from the bag and placed the buttery stack on a paper plate. Then he pushed it toward her. She stared down at it.

"Thank you." She smiled. Johnson held his bottle toward her and clanked it against her.

"Cheers!" He threw his drink down his throat. Rachel took a swig of the cold beer, leaned on the chair and closed her eyes. Johnson's eyes wandered over her face and then dropped down. Her fabulous face and body somehow turned him in to a horrible burden. Only a saint, a homosexual or a eunuch would have been able to resist her carnal charms!

Rachel opened her eyes and saw him staring at her breast with gaped mouth. She tossed a shy smile at him and dug her fingers in to the pancake. She began to eat it with relish.

"You are wonderful, Rachel." She heard his voice. The drink had made his voice unsteady. Rachel stopped eating and took another nip from the beer.

'' Johnson, I knew all you guys. Some kind of nerds!'',She began to giggle, "And you are a heated up voyeur. You agree?"

"Of course, I agree. And as for me, you are a clever vixen!" Johnson chuckled, ran out of breath and picked up the beer bottle. Then he completely drained it down his throat at a draught. Rachel bit her lips, sneaked a glance at him and continued eating. Rachel swiped her lips with butter cream and smacked them, flashing a quick smile at him.

"Hey, dude, why don't you join me. Eat a piece of the cake." She pushed the paper plate toward him. Johnson took her hand. Rachel tried to twist her hand form his grasp.

"Rachel, darling. Do you think that I am a psycho or something?" He asked as he released her hand.

"Of course, you are a psycho who's obsessed with sex.." She laughed.

"Really? Then I am going to take you in a hidden layer to fuck you until you scream. Okay?" Johnson got in his feet with an undercurrent, a sort of hum of sexual tension heated through him. With unsteady steps he swayed toward her.

Rachel took a huge gulp of beer and stared at him. Her lips were parted and her eyes reflected terror. Suddenly she got in her feet and scampered a few steps back. Johnson moved forward and tugged at her rob. She gave him a playful push. Johnson laughed, allowed him to be pushed off, but before he caught her hand and brought it to his lips.

"I am sorry. Did I scare you?." He asked, panting heavily.

"Yeah, My whole body just kind a froze up!" She cried..Then he pulled her tighter to him and wrapped one arm around her waist. His heavy breathing came over her face. Then he kissed her on the lips. Her bottom sank on the table as he deepened the kiss. Slowly he tore his mouth from hers and whispered against her ear.

"Rachel, take this robe off so I can touch and feel all over you…" Rachel's heart raced and she felt that she was falling for him. She could feel emotion tightening her throat. She couldn't frown, but a flicker of dismay touched her face.

Suddenly she heard hasty footsteps on the stairs followed by the rustling of silk dress, and then a feminine voice. Rachel gave a startled cry and sprang back as Johnson thought was fear. She was shocked, numb and in dismay. Johnson rushed to the door, shoved the door open and took several gulps of cold air.

He saw Nancy in the middle of the staircase, hands on her hips, and looking confused. He suffered torments of shame and fear and imagined whether she knew that he had just embraced and kissed Rachel. He tried to smile at Nancy and looked round nervously.

Nancy stared at him. "Why are you here?" She asked, her stern eyes meeting his directly. He could see her gaze intensified.

"Oh, it's nothing. We have just been talking together. She's such a nice fellow and told me sedately a lot about her child hood and family...."Johnson lied for a few seconds. He was deftly pretending and everything about him seemed to be gentle and soft. All the while his face expressed a kind of indifference. Then he slowly went down the stair case in to the hall and paced up and down. ....

An icy wind was raging outside, dashing around the house with the ferocity of a wild creature, knocking at the windows and scraping at the doors and walls. The room was spellbound by this savage sound.

Suddenly Nancy started and woke up from her sleep. She stared about vacantly at the dark window. It was not dawn yet. She took a loud drawn-out yawn and got up. Then she walked toward the door and turned to look at her sleeping husband. He was curled up in bed and snoring. She groped the door jamb, opened the door and stepped outside.

The interior of the house was dark,except for the little bit of moonlight coming through the glass windows.She reached the bottom of the stairs and turned to go in to the kitchen. For a moment,she stumbled around in the kitchen,switched on the light,and went to work. The lighting cast a gleam on the stainless steel appliances,granite counter tops,ceramic floors and also, on the double ovens mounted beside the six burner stove. Nancy felt better and reached for the coffee maker..........

Johnson was fast asleep. Although he took toss and turns on the bed, he was again dreaming too! And out side, the wind howled and moaned.

In his sleepy mind's eye,he was in down stairs,with a steaming cup of coffee in hand.Then he walked out on the back to enjoy the early view of the dawn. Suddenly he heard foot steps coming down the stairs.

He remembered his proposition to his wife the night before,which she declined. Well, she now seemed to agree and she's coming down. He decided to take her up on it. He hastily went back and when she reached down the stairs,grabbed her from behind. He moved her down and held her close.

In the dark corner, she trembled at first,but after he started to caress her body,she soon slumped back against his chest. He whispered in to her ear that he had a surge of lust and he wanted her badly. She didn't say a word,but responded slowly by reaching around and wraapping her hands on his manhood.

Johnson smiled and took the cue as yes,and his hands immediately began to caress her voluptous body.She moaned and he could feel lust raked through her trembling body.She rose on her toes,brought both hands behind his head, and smothered his face with hot kisses. Finally, able to come up for breath,Johnson caught her in his arms and laid gently on the floor,slipping the night gown over and off her body. Suddenly he was amazed to see her gorgeous face in the moonlight,with perspiration broke out on her brow. It was Rachel!

Rachel gasped,heaving her chest and her naked legs wide open. An invitation that he couldn't take long in accepting! She looked so elegant in the moon light,completely naked and lying there. There was a warm smile on her luscious lips,so content and happy.

"Rachel,darling!" Johnson mumbled.He was really amazed by how calm and natural she seemed.For all the days before, she was so reluctant for having sex with him.

Johnson lay down by her and embraced her with his trembling hands. He could feel an indescribable emotion tightening his throat.

"Oh, Rachel!" He took her head and gave her a long kiss on her wet lips. Then his lips crawled over her face with kisses. Slowly ending the rain of kisses, he gently entangled her with both hands.

Her body writhed with reaction to his enfolding. Her slender hands went around his neck and drew him down on her, and he couldn't stop. He felt the hard throbbing against his cloth, seeking freedom. Then he saw her hand went down, quickly opening his fly as his sex sprang free against her. Her entire body was trembling with a warm feeling as he entered her, and he felt its reaction to him. A groan of pure pleasure came over him and he thought to himself with satisfaction.

He'd never loved a woman like Rachel; not even his wife. Now he's feeling for the first time that incredible sweetness of her body. And he decided to give her more than to take as his exquisite longing nearly accomplished...

Nancy brushed her flour-coated hands on a towel, took a flask and poured hot coffee in to a cup. She suddenly sniffed the aroma from the stove and went over to check the food in the oven. Heat reached out from the oven, singeing her for a moment. Then she abruptly put the stove off and turned round. She took the cup of coffee from the countertop and hurried out on to the hall.

A little later Nancy came upstairs and opened her bedroom door. She got in to the room sleepy eyed, her hair tousled, but all beaming and cheerful. Before her, a few feet away, Johnson was curled up against the wall, mumbling something in coherently. A flea had landed on the bridge of his nose, sucking his blood greedily. But he took no notice of it and continued to whisper an endless stream of love words. Nancy, her movement languid and lazy, walked over to the bed to wake him up.

Johnson tossed over the bed, still dreaming and murmuring. He was also smiling and then his smile changed in to a wide grin.

"Oh, Rachel, My darling! I love you!" He murmured as if a tremor ran through his body. All Nancy could hear was the love words, endearments he blurted out shamelessly to her guest, Rachel. A feeling of anger and betrayal coursed through her and her whole figure expressed extreme bafflement.

"You fucking snake, are you dreaming to get another notch on your belt? Are you not ashamed?"

Outraged and anger rolled blindly over her, Nancy threw the cup of coffee against the wall. It landed in broken pieces with a loud clatter on the ceramic wall beside the bed. Then she stretched both hands, grabbed a pillow and edged forward. Her lips came off her even white teeth in a snarl as she dealt blows all over his body. As she lashed out fiercely, Johnson startled to wake up, opened his bleary eyes in wonder. For a moment he stared fearfully at the ceiling.

"What the hell?" He screamed He turned his head and caught a glimpse of Nancy's trembling, enraged figure. Her roaring stabbed at his guts. He sprang to his feet and jumped out of the bed before she thumped him on the back. As he wavered, Nancy seized him by the shoulder and threw him out of the room. Johnson's head banged on the doorpost and he fell face down on the floor. He cried aloud in the shock at the realization……..

CHAPTER 3

SLANDER ON HIS WEDDING ANNIVERSARY

Nancy was slowly climbing the staircase with bed coffee in her hand. When she heard a loud scream of her husband in the bed room, she was momentarily shocked and astonished. She rushed up the stairs and headed to the bedroom. She saw Johnson lying in the middle of the room with his face down on the floor. She was staggered by the sight of him, lying apparently unconscious by falling heavily down from the bed. Nancy was startled with terror, went white in the face and ran toward him with a loud moan. She quickly sank down beside him, putting the cup of coffee down, and turned him over. Then she bent down and looked at his fear distorted face with clouded eyes.

"Good heavens! You are not unconscious." She wailed, totally confused and uncomprehending what had happened to Johnson.

Johnson's bleary eyes moved from left to right, then focused on her face. For a moment he surveyed her face, ground his teeth and mumbled something incoherently.

Nancy huddled close to him and looked at his blurred eyes, her face ravage with suffering.

"Johnson, tell me, what's happened?" Nancy asked bursting in to tears.

"Nancy I had... I had an excruciating night mare.."

"...And I..And I fell..." He muttered in horror, moving away from the floor. He slowly rose to his feet. He was shivering and he felt his heart stood still, and his legs buckled under him as if at a terrible foreboding. His eyes were staring and he tried to say something to Nancy. But breathlessness and agitation prevented him.

He pulled himself together and sank back in to the bed. For some time, Johnson sat motionless, his head supported on his fists and wincing inwardly.

"You look so worried. Have a drink of coffee." Nancy gave him a strained smile and held out bed coffee to him. With trembling hands he took the cup of coffee and drank swiftly, throwing it down his throat. Some color flooded back his pale face. As he swallowed, he felt the mouthful was falling down the gullet as if in to a kind of abyss. He smacked his lips now and again and brought himself to say something to Nancy.

For a moment Johnson stirred restlessly and fought himself to return to reality. Amazingly, he could find out that he was relaxed and the last horrible traces of the dream were gone.

"Johnson, may I call the doctor?" Nancy asked.

"No, dear. I would like some Aspirin. I feel a terrible head ache…"Johnson replied, blinking his eyes.

"Is it a terrible kind of head ache?" Nancy asked softly as she walked over to the side of the table.

"Not that much terrible." He smiled. Nancy brought him aspirin pills and turned toward the door.

"You take rest. I am going to bring a glass of water." She said, looking back at him while crossing the door.

A little later, Nancy came with a glass of water filled with ice cubes. She sat opposite him and lifted the huge glass of water toward him. Johnson took the glass with his both hands and swallowed the pill, returning her smile with appreciation.

Johnson stared at Nancy, his mind overwhelmed with gratitude. In the clear light of the morning, there wasn't a trace of line on her face. Her eyes were clear and dark. Her wavy brown hair was secured neatly behind her head in to a kind of knot.

Johnson felt a feeling of remorse rise up inside him that he had never felt before.

"I am sorry,Nancy." He mumbled. Something in his voice made her look searchingly at him.

"What's this Johnson? Why do you feel sorry about?" Nancy snapped as she suddenly came over the side of his bed. A puzzled look came in to Johnson's eyes.

"I meant I am sorry to disturb you this morning…"He went on and cleared his throat, trying to shrug off his tenseness.

"Don't be silly, darling." Nancy forced a breezy smile and smacked a kiss on his cheek.

Johnson laughed and pulled her in to his lap. He cradled her head against his chest, leaned down and rested his chin on her hair. Slowly he nuzzled the side of her neck, nipping his way up to the sensitive shell of her ear.

"Oh, darling! It's beyond me!" Nancy squirmed and laughed.

Then Johnson ran a hand through her dark brown hair and unintentionally ruffled it.

"Oh, please stop it! You must come on down. I got breakfast." Nancy mumbled as she couldn't stop the pleasure flooding her heart. She reached for his hands that encircled her and gently twisted on them.

"Yes," He agreed. "Let's go down stairs." Johnson released her and got in to his feet. He made his way toward down stairs, followed by Nancy.

While climbing down the stairs and side stepping Nancy, Johnson felt himself guilty.

"why don't I take care of my business, without watching her guest like a pervert? Hell, I must take things seriously.."Johnson thought with repentance as he furtively cast a look at his wife's joyous face. He put an arm through her and silently walked down toward the dining room.

The sun had already risen and the golden rays pierced the whole room through the high windows. Johnson went in to the bath room and busily engaged in his morning routine. A little later he came in to the kitchen with a tooth brush in his hand. Watching the trees rising behind the kitchen and the garden path, he walked out of the back door.

In the garden, the spaces between the trees and clumps of bushes were filled with a thin, gentle mist, suffused with the light of the morning sun. Idly brushing his teeth, he walked through the garden path.

The early sun hung high above the garden, while beneath it were transparent patches of clouds streaming eastward across the sky. Far from the garden gate, a pebbled pathway ran down to the river, its bank, along the very edge of the water jagged with low bushes. The opposite bank was lost in darkness and mist with clumps of tall bushes and trees with their low drooping branches. A bird was loudly trilling its song in one of the bushes.

When Johnson walked over to the garden gate, a shadow detached itself from the mist and went towards him.

"Ah, Rachel! Why you are here? So early?" He cried in delight.

"No, Johnson. Not so early. It's past eight thirty now. I went two kilometers hiking alone and got back through the river bank…" Rachel smiled, pointing toward the river bank. Then she blew a steamy sigh on a lock of hair escaping from her tousled hair that fell over her forehead. Johnson's lustful eyes inspected her from head to toe.

Her long curly taffy-brown hair hung like a curtain down her waist. Her exotic face with high cheek bones was flushed. Beads of perspiration were clung on to her face. She was wearing a loose fitting, blue flannel shirt that buttoned in the front. Her long, lithe legs were in tight black jeans. Lumps of clay were clung to her hiking boots.

Rachel gave him a beguiling smile and stood shadowed by the bushes. She seemed to him a lovely, lonely creature. As she stretched and took turns, he didn't move, thinking for the first time he had seen her in the summer house. He also thought about the lustful scenes in his dreams. It had all seemed a shame to him and no fault of his own.

"How's the hiking in the wee hours of dawn?" Johnson asked as they passed the garden gate toward the yard.

"Not so bad at all. I was really enjoying, except those slippery, bogey ground by the sloping bank. The final trudge up the slope was tiring…" Her voice was so sweet and he saw her eyes twinkled.

"Rachel, you are one of the bravest girls in the hill station, a daring Siren!.." Johnson hesitated in mid sentence. "And you look so damned pretty!" He finished in sibilant whisper. Johnson saw her eyes shadowed now.

"Johnson! I don't like such comments." Rachel raised her voice in protest. Her cool, unafraid voice disconcerted him. He rolled his eyes in embarrassment. With flushed face, Rachel turned and waddled toward the porch.

Johnson watched her with his eyes glittering and grimaced. Suddenly a news paper boy peddled a bicycle along the road, loudly jingling the bell, his back seat loaded with the bundle. He stopped at the gate, threw a news paper in front of Johnson and turned round. He shuffled his legs restlessly and sped speedily down the lane. Ahead of him, and along the long fence, everything was hidden by a haze.

Johnson picked up the news paper and glanced up at Rachel. Holding the news paper in one hand and pressing a finger against his chin he wondered, then laughed aloud. He was glowing indeed and his whole appearance exuded happiness.

"God! Imagine my predicament! Ha-ha!" He laughed and gasped.

"That jelly belly is something; and she doesn't like flirting! Whenever I try to stick her like a fly to a fly mesh, she grumbles! Oh my God, look at her swaying back! The sight of her magnificent butt alone sends more blood to my loins!"

Johnson grinned fixedly, his face flushed with desire for her. Although he was just having fun, he was sure one thing about Rachel. She had what so ever no inclination to have an affair with a happily married man like him.

"Rachel, my baby, you want some loving! And I am the only guy in this hill station to give it to you…" He gasped with laughter.

Johnson, all the while, thought that she would better have a wild affair with somebody in a strange city some thousand miles away, than to him. She's really something, but pretending a career –driven workaholic woman before him. Pretending to be so frigid and fairly constant to her occupation! Alas, for him, there's no chance to put some excitement and adventure back in to his bored life!

"She's really the only striking belle in the hill station. A classical profile with enormous dark eyes! A firm, voluptuous body with a thick plait of brown curls down to her waist! Well, I guess, who would be terribly lucky in love with her!"

Johnson muttered, flushing purple and glaring at a stray dog that sniffed at the corners of the garden. The dog walked listlessly toward him, wagged its tail, growled and sniffed at his legs.

Johnson gave a start, jumped a few paces back, and issued a wild, piercing cry which made the dog jump on all four paws. The dog felt even more terrified, showed its teeth and snarled. Johnson turned round and sauntered toward the yard. Looking back, he saw the dog reared up on its hind legs and gnashing its teeth, uttering rasping cries. Johnson started again, went white in the face and as if seized with horror, dashed headlong toward the house like a mad man.

It was toward nine'0 clock in the morning. They were all sitting round the dining table for breakfast. The dining room, with pale blue walls and rose wood work, was furnished with a round table and wing chairs.

There was a cautious aloofness about Johnson, and he had a wary smile on his face. The breakfast was delicious. Nancy busily engaged to serve food. She found Rachel warm and charming, James nibbling at the plate and breaking jokes, and Johnson somewhat withdrawn.

They started with crisp *chapatis* and potato curry and followed that with chilly chicken and cheese *tartlets* for dessert.

James was thoughtful for a moment.

"Aunty, look at your husband. Why does he keep reticent all the while?" He said dryly, looking askance at Johnson." You know, it's like sitting near a volcano, waiting for it to erupt! You never know when it's going to happen…"

Johnson felt a sharp sense of shame. "James, mind your words! Stop this stupid conversation.." Johnson blurted out angrily, leaned forward, and banged his fist on the table. James suddenly cringed, feeling that his uncle's dignity outraged at his words.

"Ah, it's erupting! Aunty, look at him. He's shouting and is on the verge of throwing tantrums!" James flushed and blinked as if fearfully.

"James!" Johnson said sternly, taking him by the arm and squeezing it.

"You must keep up the table manners."

James went pale. "Uncle, but my intentions are not to disgrace you. It's honorable.."

Johnson stared at James, his, mouth wide open, and eyes bulging, just like a big question mark.

"Uncle, I can understand your feelings. Please calm down. I am just joking.."James mumbled.

Rachel looked at both of them in astonishment and shrugged her shoulders.

"Nancy, I don't know why they are making such a fuss about.." She said to Nancy. They exchanged glances and laughed.

"Oh, dear, they are so stupid. It's really immature and silly. I just don't know what to say. "Nancy replied, waving her arms about, and then she turned to James.

"James, you would better be quiet and stop offending the air with that pricking tongue of yours. Remember, if you were in Johnson's place, you would rather be boiled alive with shame…"She burst out laughing.

Johnson looked at his wife in dismay, and then his eyes roved over Rachel's face. With her left hand she was straightening her collar and her big lustrous eyes held on his gaze. Suddenly Nancy interrupted.

"By the way, Johnson, can you remember the importance of next Saturday?" She was spacing out the syllables importantly, stepping his side with a large dish. Johnson looked at her curiously. He tried to remember for a moment, and then shyly tugging at his moustache, and keeping his eyes downcast, he said.

"I am sorry Nancy, I can't remember. What's it?"

Nancy wrinkled her brow in puzzlement. "Oh, Jeez! He can't even remember his wedding anniversary! What a plight!"Nancy exclaimed in a sharp, unpleasant feeling of sadness. But she could still see a wistful, warm, sentimental mood spread out on Johnson's flushed face.

Suddenly James said, bursting out laughing. "Aunty, My uncle actually think that he would be damned, if he exactly knew the date of his wedding anniversary.."

Johnson growled as if again suddenly ashamed and waved his arms. He took a glass and gulped down the water.

"Oh, James, are you crazy? It's just like stabbing him in the side with a blunt dagger.."Rachel said hoarsely.

"Oh, then I am sorry uncle."James mumbled, "I behaved so foolishly and I confess, as a gentleman…"

"Well, James, I accept your apology. You should never behave tactlessly before elders.." Johnson said weakly. His eyes had a dull expression and his red nose shone in the light.

"Certainly, uncle." James said, agreeing and blinking his eyes contritely with a smile.

"Oh, my God!, James apologized and humbled himself. What a surprise! Rachel, will he now go down on his knees before Johnson? Look at his face; there's still tears glistening on his eye lashes.'" Nancy burst into loud laughter.

Ashamed and perplexed, James leapt to his feet and quickly started toward the wash base.

"Aunty, that's enough! Yet,you know that I am a pathetic hanger-on who's confined here with a kind of noble, exalted slavery. And I did apologize from an awful muddle that suddenly accumulated in my head. That's all …"

James spoke aloud, staring before the mirror with intensity, while washing his hands.

"Yeah! That's a kind of magnanimous endurance and extraordinary resignation to fate my lad! I love you!" Nancy replied through peals of laughter.

Rachel slowly rose to her feet, made a step toward James and stared in to his face. He appeared crazed, but she sensed so much beauty in the fire burning in his eyes. She stood transfixed by him, patting on his back and staring rapturously on his face.

'Oh, Rachel! Take me in to your hands, "James said, suddenly stretching his hands to her, and assuming a pleading expression, "I am disgraced. Please console me!"

"But James my hands are dirty. I advise you just wait. I mean, until you fall in love with someone. She will surely bring you the warmth of her affection and even cuddle you whenever you feel bothered about something …."Rachel drawled.

She stood so sweet, framed in the seductive light in the corner of the room.

"Clever talk!" James released a pent-up breath and his face darkened. He watched her curly hair started to crawl around her beautiful, smiling face.

She made him feel relaxed and he suddenly felt a smile curve on his lips.

The days passed swiftly. On the Saturday evening, Johnson was celebrating his wedding anniversary in grand style. His sprawling two storey house, huddled between pine trees in a square plot, at the slope of the hill, was crowded with so many family friends and relatives. After seven 0' clock the other guests began to arrive for the dinner party. There were more than thirty people, and all of them were either Nancy's colleagues or their neighbors. There were gifts from every guest and they swarmed round them exchanging hellos. They greeted the couple and the joy of being with such friendly people was immense for them. The wedding anniversary festivities went on smoothly; and the evening was warm and pleasant.

Nancy moved around the guests happily in a vintage gray ball gown, with diamonds gleaming at her ears, neck and wrists. Her skin still shone in the light like a damsel in her twenties. She wore her hair long and loose, another girlish touch that belied her age.

Rachel was also along with Nancy, talking pleasantly all the time to the guests. Her soft brown hair swayed, caressed and shimmered around her flawless face. Her outfit was pretty good looking. She was clad in a silk halter top. Her waist was tiny and her belly button winked erotically between the bottom of her halter and the top of her long skirt.

James looked at the guests and then at the exquisitely decorated drawing room.

"Too many people,and too many flowers! It looks like somebody died!"He scowled, looking at the hostess.

At the end of the spacious hall, in front of the row of guests, a concert was playing, displaying the sort of instinctive virtuosity. The bright light falling down from the chandelier played cheerfully on the faces of the guests.

The guests were sitting on arm chairs, mesmerized at the beauty and grace of the conductor at the piano stool. It seemed the conductor had no idea how long he had been playing. The music had transported him in to a trance-like state, where time and place dissolved.

Bustling to and fro in the other rooms were service boys in black suit and ties, serving drinks and snacks to the guests. They were hired from a renowned star hotel in the city. The rooms were filled with a constant hubbub of conversation.

Exactly at eight 0' clock, Johnson, the anxious host went in to the kitchen to see everything was ready for the dinner. The Main cook, Stella Mathews, was all alone in the kitchen. She was a snub nosed woman with a huge stomach.

The large kitchen was redolent from floor to ceiling with the swirling smoke of roasted meat, chicken and much else. The food items and drinks were set out on the counter tops and a table in artistic disarray.

Stella was busy at the table. Johnson knew that she was a cook expert, who had been appreciated by many, for trying some of those new recipes she had downloaded off the computer. She was standing near the tiled counter top, arrayed with stain-less steel appliances and a pair of hand embroidered kitchen towels.

"wow! What a fragrance! I could eat the whole kitchen!"Johnson laughed low and padded in to the kitchen.

"Come on, Stella, show me the dishes!"

Stella smiled at Johnson, dropped her arms to her sides and stepped around him happily.

"Come on Stella, first show the roasted meat…"Johnson said, rubbing his hands and licking his lips.

Stella went up to the counter top and carefully lifted a greased sheet. Under it, on an enormous dish, laid big, roasted pieces of meat, garnished with onion and carrot chips. Johnson looked at those items with relish and gasped. His face beamed and his eyes rolled. He went over closely, and made his lips a noise like that of a loud smacking kiss. After standing there for a moment, he turned to Stella, snapped his fingers with delight and smacked his lips loudly again.

"Ah, the sound of a passionate kiss! Who are you kissing Stella?" Came a voice from the next room and suddenly, in the doorway appeared the head of James.

"Who is it? You are!" James bewildered as he stepped in. He flushed for a moment and then smiled at Johnson.

"Ah, Uncle! It's you! A pleasure! There's still a fine old boy for you, to put it mildly!" James burst out laughing.

Johnson was aghast, he went pale in the face, and he felt his heart breaking in itty-bitty pieces.

"I am... I am.. Not kissing at all!"Johnson replied, embarrassed.

"Who gave you that Idea, you fool! It was I..Well... just smacking my lips in token of delight at the sight of the cooked meat and other delicious delicacies..."

"Ha! Ha! Uncle, tell me another lie!" James grinned from ear to ear, and before Johnson could retort, he vanished out of the door. Johnson flushed.

Stella sniggered, and swaying side by side, retreated back a cardboard screen that cordoned off from the rest of the kitchen. Johnson could still hear her peals of laughter. He buckled under the pressure of the incident, and went shaky at the knees with a kind of foreboding. It seemed the whole evening and the celebration itself had turned out a nightmare; a fitting end to one of the worst days of his life.

"Dammit!" Johnson thought, "Now that nephew of me will go in to the main hall and start gossiping. He will blacken my name all over here, the rogue.."

Johnson went timidly in to the hall room and glanced round. He stared at the guests, his mind blank.

"Where is James?"

Then he saw him standing near the piano and bending over, whispering something to a stout man. He was a gentle, mild mannered person and very friendly to Johnson. He was Mr. David, a doctor working at Blue hill Hospital and a neighbor to him. Now Johnson could see Mr. David turn and blew a disdainful smoke ring toward his direction.

"My God! It's all about me!", Johnson thought in dismay. "James talked to him everything, blast him! And David believes him! Now David stopped smoking. He's looking at me and laughing!"

Johnson grunted and pushed his way through the guests toward David.

"Ah! I can't leave it at like that! No! At any cost, I must make sure David doesn't believe him..." Johnson scratched his head in a hurry, still embarrassed, and went up to Doctor David.

"Doctor David!" Johnson said in an unnaturally husky voice.

"Hello, Johnson, where have you been all the while? I suppose you have been secretly boozing in the kitchen..."

"Hrrmph!" Johnson mumbled, "There has been a trouble. You know, doctor, I have been giving instructions to Stella, the cook, about the dinner party. And, by the way, I nearly forgot myself when I saw the meat dish. I looked at it and out of pleasure..Out of pure delight, I smacked my lips, when suddenly that James came in."

Doctor David laughed and looked somewhere to one side.

"David, please listen to me..." Johnson asked with a pleading expression.

"And James, that scoundrel, says, 'Ah, uncle, are you kissing in here'. With whom do you think? That cook, Stella. That middle aged woman, with a repulsive and abnormally fat body. Fancy thinking that; the foolish fellow, my nephew! He makes out that I have been kissing her! The crank!"

"Who's the crank? Tell me Johnson..."Asked a friend of Johnson as he came up. It was Philip, a famous criminal lawyer in his early thirties who's been practicing at the high court. He was an intelligent looking man with an engaging boyishness about him.

"Him over there, James!" You know Philip, I go in..in to the kitchen, I mean..."

Johnson told all about James to Philip as well.

"Isn't it silly of him, the crank? Truly, I'd rather kiss the dog than that fat, ungainly Stella" Added Johnson. As he looked round he saw, Mr. Stephan, another neighbor standing behind him.

"Hello, Stephan, we were talking about James, my nephew "He explained everything to Stephan in a hurry.

"James comes in to the kitchen and he sees me beside Stella, the cook. And..and he went thinking up all kinds of jokes. 'What, kissing are you?'He says. You know, it must have been the hot drink that made him imagine it.

So, I say I would rather kiss the dog than Stella. Besides, I say, I have a wife, your aunty. And what a fool you are...."

"Who's the fool?" Asked another guest, as he came up.

"James, who else? You know, I am just standing in the kitchen, looking at an enormous dish of roasted meat..."And so on! In less than half an hour almost all of the guests had heard the story of James and the meat dish.

After a while, releasing a loud breath, and almost fatigued, Johnson slowly went in to a living room and sat comfortably at an inlaid table.

"Now, let James tell story to all of them!"Thought Johnson, rubbing his hands and smiling..

"Just let him! He will start telling them and they will say loudly, 'That's enough of your nonsense, you fool! We already know the whole story!' They would say.."

As he thought and relaxed Rachel came and stopped at the doorway. There was a look of surprise on her face. Johnson smiled at her and looked at her curiously. She was wearing a silk halter top and a matching skirt that was gathered at her waist below the belly button by a golden girdle. There was a pert thrust of her breasts against the silk halter top as she moved briskly toward him. She was carrying a pitcher of water and a glass.

"Hello, Johnson, I thought you might need this."She smiled as she set the pitcher and glass on the table.

"Thank you, Rachel." Johnson filled the glass and swallowed the water in one head-tilted back gesture. He felt so thirsty that he drank four many glasses, too many out of sheer joy. Then he coughed, leaned back in the stiff chair, and looked Rachel through teary eyes. He found Rachel so attractive in her cute outfit. He saw her sensuous lips twitched in a way real pouty. He liked her soft lips.

"Oh I wish if those blossoming lips were colored with blood-red lipstick, like a cloak!"He thought.

"Rachel, how pretty you are today "He whispered with a broad grin. Suddenly, Rachel flashed a great, pixie smile at him.

"Johnson, I have heard some small talk about you. Is it true?"Rachel asked curiously, still watching the glances he kept throwing at her. She was convinced that he had a story to tell, something necessary, ticklish and unpleasant.

Rachel sat upright in a chair near him, with her legs extended and her feet a little apart. She was wearing black stiletto heels on her feet. Then she placed her hands on the hem of her skirt and slowly tugged it upward to her knees, showing her manicured toes. She looked so sexy to him. A crazy thought passed through his mind.

"Wow, she's mind blowing! What if I pull her up and slip an arm under the hem of her skirt..And… and.. Caress her bottom!"

Johnson issued a deep sigh and told Rachel the whole story and almost apologetically begged her not to tell anything to Nancy. Rachel seemed remote with intermittent, scarcely, perceptible flutter of her long, black eyelashes, as he related the details in the kitchen.

Finally, Rachel rose to her feet and started for the door, gliding past him on her firm, lithe legs. Johnson could still smell the lingering, erotic scent of her perfume as she went past him,. Rachel stayed for a moment at the door. He leaned back in the chair and reached for a cigarette from the box on the table. Thoughtfully, he stared at Rachel and saw her glancing back at him. He couldn't take his eyes off her deep, lustrous eyes. The cigarette hung in his lips unlit as she said awkwardly.

"Johnson, we have got many guests up here. Why don't you come and join with them?"

"I will come after a drag.." He smiled.

"Well, Johnson, you please excuse me. This is none of my business, but even so I have to make it clear. You see, there are rumors going around that you have an affair with the cook. But I honestly believe your confession and consider this only a stupid gossip. But you just tell me one thing. Why can't you remain content with your wife's love and fidelity? I fancy that you are going to be unfaithful to her, and often fail to create a tempo that matched to her heart…"

Johnson's mouth twitched sideways, his chin trembled and he blinked in embarrassment. He picked out the cigarette from his lips with his stiff fingers and stared at her.

"Rachel, this is all rubbish! I love my wife so passionately, and she's dearer to me than life; than my own salvation! Are you just joking, or..Serious?" Johnson looked at her in bewilderment and spread out his arms in a strange gesture.

"Okay, Johnson, I trust you. I am not joking either. Well, allow me to leave.."Rachel smiled, nodded her head, and walked out with a muffled laughter.

When Rachel had left him alone, Johnson struck a match and held it to his cigarette. For some time, he sat fidgeting in his chair, staring up at the ceiling, and blowing coils of smoke.

At the dinner party, Johnson was red faced and grave, keeping silent all the while. His bleary eyes seemed rather moving warily over the hanging festoons and the bespangled walls in the hall, than at the smiling faces of the guests. And he pretended not to be listening to the guests who were constantly disturbing the peace with their dinnertime chatter. He fancied that the noisy guests were more likely a flock of colorful storks which had suddenly alighted to rest on his hall and dining room during their migration. As he fully engrossed eating, and glancing round, he caught Nancy's eyes. At first her eyes seemed flaring up, then suddenly there was a look of contempt, that was soon replaced by a grimly look. He found out that she was not at all in a splendid mood either to the guests. Looking up at her searing eyes again, he pissed off and cowered like a frozen lamb.

After the noisy dinner party, and escorting the guests at the main gate, Johnson hurriedly went in to his room and fell asleep like a perfectly innocent boy.

By the next morning, he had already forgotten the business with the meat dish in the kitchen. After eight o' clock, and Scrambling down the staircase, he came in to dining room for breakfast. He greeted Rachel and sat down at the table opposite her. He could see James flushed and perched on the edge of a chair beside her.

In a desperate attempt to cover up his awkwardness and conceal a kind of struggle taken place him, James gave his uncle a strained smile and wished him 'good morning'.

Johnson felt disgusted. When he met Nancy's gaze, he was even more annoyed and felt himself a silly fool. While eating, Nancy gave him a prolonged, horrible stare. Johnson recoiled, and from deep down in the depth of his soul, he sensed an incomprehensible, terrible fright overwhelmed him.

"Why aren't you eating anything?"Asked Nancy, frowning for a second, "And what are you thinking about? Feeling heart-sick for Stella? I know all about it, you heathen!"

Johnson started. He got up from the table and not feeling the ground under his feet, made his way toward James.

"You are a scoundrel!"Johnson yelled at the top of his voice, pulling him up by the scruff of the collar, "Why did you sling all that mud at me in front of everybody? Why did you start the slander going about me?" Johnson could not contain at the wild momentum of his rage.

"What slander? Uncle, what's this all about? You are imagining things!"James screamed. His eyes reddened and filled with tears.

Rachel and Nancy exchanged glances in terror. "Johnson, this is too much! Please stop it! Won't you come back and sit down? This is terrible!" Nancy pleaded in dismay. Johnson started waving James off vigorously and he backed away from him.

"I am sorry Nancy!," He mumbled ", I almost went mad, because I am grief –stricken …"He breathed a deep sigh.

His face expressed indifference, and only at the tiny drops shining down the cheek that they could discern he was crying silently. Johnson passed a hand over his eyes, and his hand seemed to grow moist from it. He walked away from the table and gazed dull eyed around the room. Then he saw Rachel, with a surprise darted across her face, pressing a silencing finger to her lips.

After a few more steps toward James, Johnson asked to him in a lugubrious voice.

"Why did you spread that I had been kissing Stella?"

James blinked with all the fibers on his battered face. He abruptly made the sign of cross and replied emotionally. "Uncle, may god punish me if I ever said a single word about you. May I conk out and vanish from the face of this earth……"

"But who, then?" Johnson wondered, running over his mind all his acquaintances and beating his breast.

"Johnson you suspect about someone. Who would be it? You might well ask this question to yourself before you cudgel the brain! Then you can find out a convincing reply.."Rachel said ruefully.

Johnson looked at her in bewilderment, spread out his arms dismissively, and sat down at the table. A shadow fell across his face. The truth itself had begun to gnaw at his heart. And that truth was ugly and painstaking.

"Johnson, what a silly fool you are!"Nancy smiled, watching the cold sweat started on his forehead.

"Ah, that's it, Aunty. If he wants to find the person behind the gossip, He should first roll his own name on his tongue! I didn't say anything about him. You know, it's because…it's because.. I am damn sure that my uncle would rather go for an expensive cook…no..No… I mean… rather go for an expensive hooker than that dirty toad, Stella Mathews……"The words kept tumbling from James's lips in wild, disjointed sentences.

Johnson started, and turned toward James with ghastly contorted face. For a moment there ensued a dead silence. Nancy and Rachel stared at each other as if stunned. They saw Johnson's bulging eyes glittering, and slowly his face went purple. He leaned toward James and clapped lightly on the shoulder.

Suddenly he began to chortle, and his chest and stomach quivered from that, happy, tickling laughter. As if enthralled by the witticism, Nancy and Rachel also burst in to loud laughter. For some time, they could not choke back their laughter that rumbled across the table.

…And I..And I fell…" He muttered in horror, moving away from the floor. He slowly rose to his feet. He was shivering and he felt his heart stood still, and his legs buckled under him as if at a terrible foreboding. His eyes were staring and he tried to say something to Nancy. But breathlessness and agitation prevented him.

He pulled himself together and sank back in to the bed. For some time, Johnson sat motionless, his head supported on his fists and wincing inwardly.

"You look so worried. Have a drink of coffee." Nancy gave him a strained smile and held out bed coffee to him. With trembling hands he took the cup of coffee and drank swiftly, throwing it down his throat. Some color flooded back his pale face. As he swallowed, he felt the mouthful was falling down the gullet as if in to a kind of abyss. He smacked his lips now and again and brought himself to say something to Nancy.

For a moment Johnson stirred restlessly and fought himself to return to reality. Amazingly, he could find out that he was relaxed and the last horrible traces of the dream were gone.

"Johnson, may I call the doctor?" Nancy asked.

"No, dear. I would like some Aspirin. I feel a terrible head ache…"Johnson replied, blinking his eyes.

"Is it a terrible kind of head ache?" Nancy asked softly as she walked over to the side of the table.

"Not that much terrible." He smiled. Nancy brought him aspirin pills and turned toward the door.

"You take rest. I am going to bring a glass of water." She said, looking back at him while crossing the door.

A little later, Nancy came with a glass of water filled with ice cubes. She sat opposite him and lifted the huge glass of water toward him. Johnson took the glass with his both hands and swallowed the pill, returning her smile with appreciation.

Johnson stared at Nancy, his mind overwhelmed with gratitude. In the clear light of the morning, there wasn't a trace of line on her face. Her eyes were clear and dark. Her wavy brown hair was secured neatly behind her head in to a kind of knot.

Johnson felt a feeling of remorse rise up inside him that he had never felt before.

"I am sorry,Nancy." He mumbled. Something in his voice made her look searchingly at him.

"What's this Johnson? Why do you feel sorry about?" Nancy snapped as she suddenly came over the side of his bed. A puzzled look came in to Johnson's eyes.

"I meant I am sorry to disturb you this morning..."He went on and cleared his throat, trying to shrug off his tenseness.

"Don't be silly, darling." Nancy forced a breezy smile and smacked a kiss on his cheek.

Johnson laughed and pulled her in to his lap. He cradled her head against his chest, leaned down and rested his chin on her hair. Slowly he nuzzled the side of her neck, nipping his way up to the sensitive shell of her ear.

"Oh, darling! It's beyond me!" Nancy squirmed and laughed.

Then Johnson ran a hand through her dark brown hair and unintentionally ruffled it.

"Oh, please stop it! You must come on down. I got breakfast." Nancy mumbled as she couldn't stop the pleasure flooding her heart. She reached for his hands that encircled her and gently twisted on them.

"Yes," he agreed. "Let's go down stairs."Johnson released her and got in to his feet. He made his way toward down stairs, followed by Nancy.

While climbing down the stairs and side stepping Nancy, Johnson felt himself guilty.

"why don't I take care of my business, without watching her guest like a pervert? Hell, I must take things seriously.."Johnson thought with repentance as he furtively cast a look at his wife's joyous face. He put an arm through her and silently walked down toward the dining room.

The sun had already risen and the golden rays pierced the whole room through the high windows. Johnson went in to the bath room and busily engaged in his morning routine. A little later he came in to the kitchen with a tooth brush in his hand. Watching the trees rising behind the kitchen and the garden path, he walked out of the back door.

In the garden, the spaces between the trees and clumps of bushes were filled with a thin, gentle mist, suffused with the light of the morning sun. Idly brushing his teeth, he walked through the garden path.

The early sun hung high above the garden, while beneath it were transparent patches of clouds streaming eastward across the sky. Far from the garden gate, a pebbled pathway ran down to the river, its bank, along the very edge of the water jagged with low bushes. The opposite bank was lost in darkness and mist with clumps of tall bushes and trees with their low drooping branches. A bird was loudly trilling its song in one of the bushes.

When Johnson walked over to the garden gate, a shadow detached itself from the mist and went towards him.

"Ah, Rachel! Why you are here? So early?" He cried in delight.

"No, Johnson. Not so early. It's past eight thirty now. I went two kilometers hiking alone and got back through the river bank…" Rachel smiled, pointing toward the river bank. Then she blew a steamy sigh on a lock of hair escaping from her tousled hair that fell over her forehead. Johnson's lustful eyes inspected her from head to toe.

Her long curly taffy-brown hair hung like a curtain down her waist. Her exotic face with high cheek bones was flushed. Beads of perspiration were clung on to her face. She was wearing a loose fitting, blue turtle neck flannel shirt that buttoned in the front. Her long, lithe legs were in tight black jeans. Lumps of clay were clung to her hiking boots.

Rachel gave him a beguiling smile and stood shadowed by the bushes. She seemed to him a lovely, lonely creature. As she stretched and took turns, he didn't move, thinking for the first time he had seen her in the summer house. He also thought about the lustful scenes in his dreams. It had all seemed a sham to him and no fault of his own.

"How's the hiking in the wee hours of dawn?" Johnson asked as they passed the garden gate toward the yard.

"Not so bad at all. I was really enjoying, except those slippery, bogey ground by the sloping bank. The final trudge up the slope was tiring…" Her voice was so sweet and he saw her eyes twinkled.

"Rachel, you are one of the brave girls in the hill station, a daring Siren!.." Johnson hesitated in mid sentence. "And you look so damned pretty!" He finished in sibilant whisper. Johnson saw her eyes shadowed now.

"Johnson! I don't like such comments." Rachel raised her voice in protest. Her cool, unafraid voice disconcerted him. He rolled his eyes in embarrassment. With flushed face, Rachel turned and waddled toward the porch.

Johnson watched her with his eyes glittering and grimaced. Suddenly a news paper boy peddled a bicycle along the road, loudly jingling the bell, his back seat loaded with the bundle. He stopped at the gate, threw a news paper in front of Johnson and turned round. He shuffled his legs restlessly and sped speedily down the lane. Ahead of him, and along the long fence, everything was hidden by a haze.

Johnson picked up the news paper and glanced up at Rachel. Holding the news paper in one hand and pressing a finger against his chin he wondered, then laughed aloud. He was glowing indeed and his whole appearance exuded happiness.

"God! Imagine my predicament! Ha-ha!" He laughed and gasped.

"That jelly belly is something; and she doesn't like flirting! Whenever I try to stick her like a fly to a fly mesh, she grumbles! Oh my God, look at her swaying back! The sight of her magnificent butt alone sends more blood to my loins!"

Johnson grinned fixedly, his face flushed with desire for her. Although he was just having fun, he was sure one thing about Rachel. She had what so ever no inclination to have an affair with a happily married man like him.

"Rachel, my baby, you want some loving! And I am the only guy in this hill station to give it to you…" He gasped with laughter.

Johnson, all the while, thought that she would better have a wild affair with somebody in a strange city some thousand miles away, than to him. she's really something, but pretending a career –driven workaholic woman before him. Pretending to be so frigid and fairly constant to her occupation! Alas, for him, there's no chance to put some excitement and adventure back in to his bored life!

"She's really the only striking belle in the hill station. A classical profile with enormous dark eyes! A firm, voluptuous body with a thick plait of brown curls down to her waist! Well, I guess, who would be terribly lucky in love with her!"

Johnson muttered, flushing purple and glaring at a stray dog that sniffed at the corners of the garden. The dog walked listlessly toward him, wagged its tail, growled and sniffed at his legs.

Johnson gave a start, jumped a few paces back, and issued a wild, piercing cry which made the dog jump on all four paws. The dog felt even more terrified, showed its teeth and snarled. Johnson turned round and sauntered toward the yard. Looking back, he saw the dog reared up on its hind legs and gnashing its teeth, uttering rasping cries. Johnson went started again, went white in the face and as if seized with horror, dashed headlong toward the house like a mad man.

It was toward 9'0 clock in the morning. They were all sitting round the dining table for breakfast. The dining room, with pale blue walls and rose wood work, was furnished with a round table and wing chairs.

There was a cautious aloofness about Johnson, and he had a wary smile on his face. The breakfast was delicious. Nancy busily engaged to serve food. She found Rachel warm and charming, James nibbling at the plate and breaking jokes, and Johnson somewhat withdrawn.

They started with crisp *chapattis* and potato curry and followed that with chilly chicken and cheese *tartlets* for dessert.

James was thoughtful for a moment.

"Aunty, look at your husband. Why does he keep reticent all the while?" He said dryly, looking askance at Johnson." You know, it's like sitting near a volcano, waiting for it to erupt! You never know when it's going to happen…"

Johnson felt a sharp sense of shame. "James, mind your words! Stop this stupid conversation.." Johnson blurted out angrily, leaned forward, and banged his fist on the table. James suddenly cringed, feeling that his uncle's dignity outraged at his words.

"Ah, it's erupting! Aunty, look at him. He's shouting and is on the verge of throwing tantrums!" James flushed and blinked as if fearfully.

"James!" Johnson said sternly, taking him by the arm and squeezing it.

"You must keep up the table manners."

James went pale. "Uncle, but my intentions are not to disgrace you. It's honorable.."

Johnson stared at James, his, mouth wide open, and eyes bulging, just like a big question mark.

"Uncle, I can understand your feelings. Please calm down. I am just joking.."James mumbled.

Rachel looked at both of them in astonishment and shrugged her shoulders.

"Nancy, I don't know why they are making such a fuss about.." She said to Nancy. They exchanged glances and laughed.

"Oh, dear, they are so stupid. It's really immature and silly. I just don't know what to say. "Nancy replied, waving her arms, and then she turned to James.

"James, you would better be quiet and stop offending the air with that pricking tongue of yours. Remember, if you were in Johnson's place, you would rather be boiled alive with shame…"She burst out laughing.

Johnson looked at his wife in dismay, and then his eyes roved over Rachel's face. With her left hand she was straightening her collar and her big lustrous eyes held on his gaze. Suddenly Nancy interrupted.

"By the way, Johnson, can you remember the importance of next Saturday?" She was spacing out the syllables importantly, stepping his side with a large dish. Johnson looked at her curiously. He tried to remember for a moment, and then shyly tugging at his moustache, and keeping his eyes downcast, he said.

"I am sorry Nancy, I can't remember. What's it?"

Nancy wrinkled her brow in puzzlement. "Oh, Jeez! He can't even remember his wedding anniversary! What a plight!"Nancy exclaimed in a sharp, unpleasant feeling of sadness. But she could still see a wistful, warm, sentimental mood spread out on Johnson's flushed face.

Suddenly James said, bursting out laughing. "Aunty, My uncle actually think that he would be damned, if he exactly knew the date of his wedding anniversary.."

Johnson growled as if again suddenly ashamed and waved his arms. He took a glass and gulped down the water.

"Oh, James, are you crazy? It's just like stabbing him in the side with a blunt dagger.."Rachel said hoarsely.

"Oh, then I am sorry uncle."James mumbled, "I behaved so foolishly and I confess, as a gentleman…"

"Well, James, I accept your apology. You should never behave tactlessly before elders.." Johnson said weakly. His eyes had a dull expression and his red nose shone in the light.

"Certainly, uncle." James said, agreeing and blinking his eyes contritely with a smile.

"Oh, my God!, James apologized and humbled himself. What a surprise! Rachel, will he now go down on his knees before Johnson? Look at his face; there's still tears glistening on his eye lashes." Nancy burst into loud laughter.

Ashamed and perplexed, James leapt to his feet and quickly started toward the wash base.

"Aunty, that's enough! Yet,you know that I am a pathetic hanger-on who's confined here with a kind of noble, exalted slavery. And I did apologize from an awful muddle that suddenly accumulated in my head. That's all …"

James spoke aloud, staring before the mirror with intensity, while washing his hands.

"Yeah! That's a kind of magnanimous endurance and extraordinary resignation to fate my lad! I love you!" Nancy replied through peals of laughter.

Rachel slowly rose to her feet, made a step toward James and stared in to his face. He appeared crazed, but she sensed so much beauty in the fire burning in his eyes. She stood transfixed by him, patting on his back and staring rapturously on his face.

'Oh, Rachel! Take me in to your hands, "James said, suddenly stretching his hands to her, and assuming a pleading expression, "I am disgraced. Please console me!"

"But James my hands are dirty. I advise you just wait. I mean, until you fall in love with someone. She will surely bring you the warmth of her affection and even cuddle you whenever you feel bothered about something …."Rachel drawled.

She stood so sweet, framed in the seductive light in the corner of the room.

"Clever talk!" James released a pent-up breath and his face darkened. He watched her curly hair started to crawl around her beautiful, smiling face.

She made him feel relaxed and he suddenly felt a smile curve on his lips.

The days passed swiftly. On the Saturday evening, Johnson was celebrating his wedding anniversary in grand style. His sprawling two storey house, huddled between pine trees in a square plot, at the slope of the hill, was crowded with so many family friends and relatives. After 7 0' clock the other guests began to arrive for the dinner party. There were more than thirty people, and all of them were either Nancy's colleagues or their neighbors. There were gifts from every guest and they swarmed round them exchanging hellos. They greeted the couple and the joy of being with such friendly people was immense for them. The wedding anniversary festivities went on smoothly; and the evening was warm and pleasant.

Nancy moved around the guests happily in a vintage gray ball gown, with diamonds gleaming at her ears, neck and wrists. Her skin still shone in the light like a damsel in her twenties. She wore her hair long and loose, another girlish touch that belied her age.

Rachel was also along with Nancy, talking pleasantly all the time to the guests. Her soft brown hair swayed, caressed and shimmered around her flawless face. Her outfit was pretty good looking. She was clad in a silk halter top. Her waist was tiny and her belly button winked erotically between the bottom of her halter and the top of her long skirt.

James looked at the guests and then at the exquisitely decorated drawing room.

"Too many people and too many flowers! It looks like somebody died!" He scowled, looking at the hostess.

At the end of the spacious hall, in front of the row of guests, a concert was playing, displaying the sort of instinctive virtuosity. The bright light falling down from the chandelier played cheerfully on the faces of the guests.

The guests were sitting on arm chairs, mesmerized at the beauty and grace of the conductor at the piano stool. It seemed the conductor had no idea how long he had been playing. The music had transported him in to a trance-like state, where time and place dissolved.

Bustling to and fro in the other rooms were service boys in black suit and ties, serving drinks and snacks to the guests. They were hired from a renowned star hotel in the city. The rooms were filled with a constant hubbub of conversation.

Exactly at eight 0' clock, Johnson, the anxious host went in to the kitchen to see everything was ready for the dinner. The Main cook, Stella Mathews, was all alone in the kitchen. She was a snub nosed woman with a huge stomach.

The large kitchen was redolent from floor to ceiling with the swirling smoke of roasted meat, chicken and much else. The food items and drinks were set out on the counter tops and a table in artistic disarray.

Stella was busy at the table. Johnson knew that she was a cook expert, who had been appreciated by many, for trying some of those new recipes she had downloaded off the computer. She was standing near the tiled counter top, arrayed with stain-less steel appliances and a pair of hand embroidered kitchen towels.

"wow! What a fragrance! I could eat the whole kitchen!"Johnson laughed low and padded in to the kitchen.

"Come on, Stella, show me the dishes!"

Stella smiled at Johnson, dropped her arms to her sides and stepped around him happily.

"Come on Stella, first show the roasted meat…"Johnson said, rubbing his hands and licking his lips.

Stella went up to the counter top and carefully lifted a greased sheet. Under it, on an enormous dish, laid big, roasted pieces of meat, garnished with onion and carrot chips. Johnson looked at those items with relish and gasped. His face beamed and his eyes rolled. He went over closely, and made his lips a noise like that of a loud smacking kiss. After standing there for a moment, he turned to Stella, snapped his fingers with delight and smacked his lips loudly again.

"Ah, the sound of a passionate kiss! Who are you kissing Stella?" Came a voice from the next room and suddenly, in the doorway appeared the head of James.

"Who is it? You are!" James bewildered as he stepped in. He flushed for a moment and then smiled at Johnson.

"Ah, Uncle! It's you! A pleasure! There's still a fine old boy for you, to put it mildly!" James burst out laughing.

Johnson was aghast, he went pale in the face, and he felt his heart breaking in itty-bitty pieces.

"I am… i am.. Not kissing at all!"Johnson replied, embarrassed.

"Who gave you that Idea, you fool! It was i..Well… just smacking my lips in token of delight at the sight of the cooked meat and other delicious delicacies…"

"Ha! Ha! Uncle, tell me another lie!" James grinned from ear to ear, and before Johnson could retort, vanished out of the door. Johnson flushed.

Stella sniggered,and swaying side by side, retreated back a cardboard screen that cordoned off from the rest of the kitchen. Johnson could still hear her peals of laughter. He buckled under the pressure of the incident, and went shaky at the knees with a kind of foreboding. It seemed the whole evening and the celebration itself had turned out a nightmare; a fitting end to one of the worst days of his life.

"Dammit!" Johnson thought, "Now that nephew of me will go in to the main hall and start gossiping. He will blacken my name all over here, the rogue.."

Johnson went timidly in to the hall room and glanced round. He stared at the guests, his mind blank.

"Where is James?"

Then he saw him standing near the piano and bending over, whispering something to a stout man. He was a gentle, mild mannered person and very friendly to Johnson. He was Mr. David, a doctor working at Blue hill Hospital and a neighbor to him. Now Johnson could see Mr. David turn and blew a disdainful smoke ring toward his direction.

"My God! It's all about me!", Johnson thought in dismay. "James talked to him everything, blast him! And David believes him! Now David stopped smoking. He's looking at me and laughing!"

Johnson grunted and pushed his way through the guests toward David.

"Ah! I can't leave it at like that! No! At any cost, I must make sure David doesn't believe him…" Johnson scratched his head in a hurry, still embarrassed, and went up to Doctor David.

"Doctor David!" Johnson said in an unnaturally husky voice.

"Hello, Johnson, where have you been all the while? I suppose you have been secretly boozing in the kitchen…"

"Hrrmph!" Johnson mumbled, "There has been a trouble. You know, doctor, I have been giving instructions to Stella, the cook, about the dinner party. And, by the way, I nearly forgot myself when I saw the meat dish. I looked at it and out of pleasure..Out of pure delight, I smacked my lips, when suddenly that James came in."

Doctor David laughed and looked somewhere to one side.

"David, please listen to me…" Johnson asked with a pleading expression.

"And James, that scoundrel, says, 'Ah, uncle, are you kissing in here'. With whom do you think? That cook, Stella. That middle aged woman, with a repulsive and abnormally fat body. Fancy thinking that; the foolish fellow, my nephew! He makes out that I have been kissing her! The crank!"

"Who's the crank? Tell me Johnson…"Asked a friend of Johnson as he came up. It was Philip, a famous criminal lawyer in his early thirties who's been practicing at the high court. He was an intelligent looking man with an engaging boyishness about him.

"Him over there, James!" You know Philip, I go in..in to the kitchen, I mean…"

Johnson told all about James to Philip as well.

"Isn't it silly of him, the crank? Truly, I'd rather kiss the dog than that fat, ungainly Stella" Added Johnson. As he looked round he saw, Mr. Stephan, another neighbor standing behind him.

"Hello, Stephan, we were talking about James, my nephew "He explained everything to Stephan in a hurry.

"James comes in to the kitchen and he sees me beside Stella, the cook. And..and he went thinking up all kinds of jokes. 'What, kissing are you?' He says. You know, it must have been the hot drink that made him imagine it. So, I say I would rather kiss the dog than Stella. Besides, I say, I have a wife, your aunty. And what a fool you are…."

"Who's the fool?" Asked another guest, as he came up.

"James, who else? You know, I am just standing in the kitchen, looking at an enormous dish of roasted meat…"And so on! In less than half an hour almost all of the guests had heard the story of James and the meat dish.

After a while, releasing a loud breath, and almost fatigued, Johnson slowly went in to a living room and sat comfortably at an inlaid table.

"Now let james tell all of them!" Thought Johnson happily,rubbing his hands

CHAPTER 4

WAGES OF SIN WRAPPED IN A BUNDLE

Blue valley hospital was an old, elegant looking white building near the residential town with an ornate lobby always crowded. The three storied, weather beaten hospital stood in the middle of a block of identical houses that set in a bowl at the feet of the mountain range. The road in front of the hospital building, which extended as far as the horizon, was flanked by towering eucalyptus trees.

It was a radiant morning. The slender tree trunks along the road took on a soft lustre of white silk as fresh snow fell before the morning sun caressed them. After the glow of dawn spread out all round, the morning sun slowly floated upward with streaks of gold stretching across the sky. The spacious hospital yard with its endless out buildings and the blooming garden were caressed by the soft sunlight.

Behind the hospital building, and some hundred meters away, there was a curve by the shore of a round lake. The clayey opposite bank of the lake, which was thickly planted with a green strip of banana, was really a beautiful view showed through the transparent veil of the mist. And beyond the banana plantation, a pine forest darkled about half a mile away. The surface of the lake, with its captivating breadth and beauty, was motionless as ever.

It was just after eight'0 clock in the morning. Dr. David was busy in his lobby before his regular rounds. He was a middle aged man with a stately imposing figure. He was a widower. His short grey beard with gold rimmed spectacles on his serious face added a kind of proud bearing.

In one hand he was holding some books tied with a string, and in the other his Stethoscope. Dr. David walked toward a filing cabinet and shoved the books inside, with a loud yawn. Then he abruptly began to search for a case file. After a moments search, he took out a file, walked back and sank in to a high backed chair.

Suddenly the telephone rang. Dr.David got up and picked up the receiver.

"Hello…yes…Is it Miss. Ann?"Dr. David's grip tightened on the telephone. He was slightly perturbed, listening, and an incredulous expression on his face. Suddenly he was in a state of shock, in complete denial what he heard from Ann Mary on the line.

"Dr. David, just you wait! I will be back and never leave you in peace. See if I don't, to teach you how to ruin innocent girls! I will leave the baby at your door step, and I will sue you, and I will… I will… tell everything to Sophia, your proud daughter….."

Dr. David nervously took a deep breath and let Miss. Ann to talk, squeezing his eyes shut tightly.

"My God! What's happening..Will Ann come over here with the baby and tell my daughter what I did to her? If she does it, Sophia would be outraged and blame me sarcastically…."

He thought agonizingly and looked down in dismay at the case file lay on the table. With a terrible feeling, he heard her out in a shock. What Miss. Ann Mary demanded was a sum of ten lakh rupees to be deposited in Axis Bank in her name. Her mind was made up.

"Mr. David, it's your flesh and blood. You see, let's not wreck the life of an innocent babe, the wages of your sin! If you are ready to deposit the amount in the bank in my name, I will never come up there. It's a word. And if you blatantly refuse, I will sue against you. I will bring shame on you. Just imagine the leering faces of your colleagues and staff. They will snigger and laugh at you…"Miss. Ann burst out angrily.

Dr.David shrank from fear and shame. "Miss. Ann, you please don't try to come over here. It's a request. Let me think it over. I will call you after a few days…"

He mumbled in trembling voice fraught with feeling. The conversation continued for some minutes. From the beginning it started as a small disagreement from Miss. Ann, and it ended up as ferocious denial as he demanded to reduce the sum to the half of it. Dr.David waited eagerly while Ann took control of herself. But he couldn't dissuade her, and feeling frustrated, he abruptly replaced the receiver.

For some time, he stood there motionless, a cynical expression on his face. Then he sat down as if stunned, and stared up, transported back to another time; and a few months ago........

Miss. Ann Mary was twenty five when he first met her. At the time she had a reputation around the hill station as a very beautiful, intelligent maid servant to a wealthy land owner. She was really more than that of a maid servant. She was a maid of honor!

Dr. David first laid his eyes on her at the church hall. The old priest, with a beaming face, introduced her to him and turning to her, acquainted him as a very distinguished and even a great man.

"Doctor, I have a favor to ask you."The priest asked to him, "Miss. Ann is a very nice young lady. She's jobless and she wants to work. Be so kind, and do her a favor…"

Dr.David looked at Ann. She was a tall, graceful brunette with regular, attractive features. Her dark eyes were full of grief, yet she kept smiling all the time and pretended to be cheerful at his presence. What Mr. David liked most in her was her naive, child like face and loving eyes.

He asked her few questions. She replied brusquely and told him everything about her in few words. A year before, she was working hard in a small farm at the valley, sending cartloads of vegetables and chicken to the market. She concluded that she could hardly feed herself on her small salary at the time. Then he asked to know how she came in to his residential town. She smiled and told him that she came up there, since a certain benefactor persuaded her to stay with him. He was a rich Tea estate owner. She subsequently told him that a few days ago her benefactor sold out the estate and went abroad with his family, literally abandoning her on the streets.

Dr. David found her words impressive and touching. Meanwhile, the church bells were ringing. He saw a dense crowd slowly coming toward the church. Faded flags, and a glittering cross soared over the crowd in front of the procession.

"Mr. David, what's your decision?"The priest asked in a hurry.

"Oh, is that all you want? It's okay. Miss. Ann can sure stay in my house."Then Mr. David turned to Miss. Ann. "We will live together a bit longer! What do you say Miss. Ann?" He asked with a flushed face.

"Mercy for the favor!" She smiled as if satisfied. The priest nodded his head and offered his hand in farewell. Then he abruptly left them, rustling his badly tailored gown that had ugly creases at the knees.

Dr.David gazed at Miss. Ann's happiness flushed face, and at her wide eyes shining with pleasure. When the church was crowded with people, Dr.David and Ann carefully pushed their way through them toward the front door.

Dr.David's mind was racing and his clouded brain was teemed with a lot of recollection from the past. Something tormented him greatly, with tiny gnawing of his conscience. His crumpled face was purple and there were beads of perspiration on his brow.

Extremely upset, he rose to his feet and left the table toward the window. He folded his arms on his chest, blinked his eyes and again lost in thoughts. He cursed the moment he took fancy at Miss. Ann, although his relation with her brought light to his long cherished clandestine desires.........

It was physically and emotionally satisfying and sometimes just downright fun. As a middle aged widower he was frustrated for years and when he was unexpectedly seduced by Miss. Ann, he found it more exciting than he ever dreamed. The relationship with her was blissfully sensual and alluringly exotic. It was just like finding new pleasures at home and he reveled in a new world of erotic delight, reaching a level of trust and comfort with her.

Dr. David recollected that over the next few days Miss. Ann was so docile, as if she had fallen in earnest to serve him with dedication. He took a tremendous liking to her. He often found her alone in the kitchen, moving busily from the six-burner stove to the fridge. She would be either balancing a carton of eggs, or a tray of vegetables, with sweat broke out on her brow. She was so pretty and looked like every man's dream. He found her voluptuous body permanently clothed in a hot looking, short Denim skirt of dark indigo with tan stitching and a matching thin cotton top. They were very trendy, particularly the cotton top which revealed her cleavage. When she turned to gaze at him, her long dark-brown hair flowed over her shoulders. Her fabulous face, her smile and sensuous body had turned him in to a horrible burden.

When they looked at each other, he could often feel a lustful spark leaped in her eyes to him. With a beaming face, she would prop her fists on her hips, watching admiringly and waiting for him to say something to her. But he often feigned to look serious and hurriedly shoved past her, controlling the feeling burgeoning within him.

One day evening, unsure of his emotions and needing time to think, Dr.David left the hospital and drove directly to his home. As he knocked Miss.Ann opened the door. He smiled and asked her how the evening went. She said 'fine' with a courteous way. Then he looked round and asked her where Sophia was. She said Sophia was visiting some of her friends and that she would be late to come home.

Dr. David sat down next to her on the couch and began to talk. It was a kind of flirting. After a while, she left him in the front room and went to take a shower. She returned about twenty minutes later, wearing a short, loose fitting silk robe. With a bewitching smile she sat next to him. Dr. David was suddenly caught up in her sheer beauty. He also suspected whether she had planned an intricate seduction in her mind. As she leaned closer toward him, he was sucked in breath as the alluring aroma of female need tickled in his nostrils. Something flared up inside him.

Dr. David saw her tingly as his wanton eyes slid over her."Ann, you look so sexy today!"He mumbled. She saw his eyes focused on the swell of her breasts, and as if in a frenzy his hands reaching out to her.

Miss. Ann licked her lips, and asked in a sweet voice, "Sir, am I really so sexy? I guess I can't really blame you if you really like me…."

She giggled and the sound of her laughter inordinately pleased and lured him. Dr. David caught her arms, leaned forward and brushed his body against the curve of her shoulder. He felt her tremble in his hands and it pleased him to know she desired him too.

Miss. Ann tossed her hair over her shoulder, laughed, and winked at him. Then she slowly pushed the blood red nails on her hair, and let her legs slide off a little. Her look was in an amorous manner. Dr.David felt his face flush as he tried not to examine her exposed creamy thighs. She was laughing all the while, and she seemed not to care that she was showing all. He gasped and gave in to temptation, and drank with his eyes the exquisite beauty between her legs. With his trembling fingers, he grabbed the hem of her robe and yanked it up. He felt her lusciously compliant. She suddenly got in her feet and let him tug it hard, until it caught around her hips. Before she raised her arms to let him remove the robe, he hastily caught her in his arms and led her toward the stairs.

"Where are you taking me?" She giggled with surprising sexuality.

"Some place to lay you…and…and climb the peaks of pleasure!" He laughed. A rush of feeling swept through his body, as she drew a deep sigh and sank her head on his shoulder.

As for Dr. David, his first casual encounter with Ann Mary was really a challenge to relax his inhibitions. He recollected that, from the beginning she was graciously obedient and later, much to his surprise, she had suddenly transformed in to a wanton siren, bringing him the delights of domination. Her efforts were dramatic and conducive enough to urge him walk on her wild side.

Dr.David restlessly paced and up and down the room and thought about his first rude encounter of deceit. And the thought of it engrossed him in grievance. There were joy, warmth and wistfulness in his heart while he lived with Miss. Ann. But the happiness she brought to him was just a simulation, her pretention to take advantage of her position. Now, even the faintest trace of her memory kept pestering him with sadness and fear.

A few months later, Miss. Ann took a bold step, crazy enough to betray him, which surprised and brought shock to him. She had already blown a lot of money that he had left for her. One day, while he was absent from his home, she robbed a wad of currency and pieces of jewelry he had kept in his chest of drawers. The currency itself was around five lakh rupees, which he considered, his entire earnings for some months.

On that fine evening, she tied up her few belonging in to a bundle, carried her baggage and listlessly walked out of his house. She had also left him a letter that she was not coming back to him anymore

When Dr.David discovered the robbery, he went terribly white in the face and collapsed in to an armchair. He couldn't believe that Miss. Ann was such a depraved and venal woman. He was thoroughly upset, he couldn't pull himself together and what decision was he to make. Finally, after so much reasoning and introspection, he sensed the truth and her state of mind. He groaned and tried to believe that it was a kind of vagrant gypsy blood in her veins that compelled more to do it. He also thought about her impoverished family in the valley and decided not to complain in the police station. He was rather like a shocked husband who was bound to feel about his cheating wife.

"It was a mistake I made! I trusted her whole heartedly!" Dr. David sighed through his tears as he raised a glass of brandy to his lips.

The next day evening, on the way to his house, he visited a familiar club in the hill station. He passed the newly decorated office in to a large, beautiful hall with rows of tables and chairs. The hall room was facing a picture window with a magnificent view of the mountain.

The club members were busily engaged playing cards by the window, wrapped in the twilight in the room. Most of them were drunken and huddled against the backs of their seats.

Dr. David came in and stopped in the middle of the room, staring hard at the club members for some time. Suddenly one of them sitting at the far end of the room exclaimed joyfully.

"Hello, Dr. David! what brings you here late at this evening? It's quite unusual, isn't it?"

It was his friend Professor. Johnson. He was looking up in surprise. He found Dr. David looking old and tired.

"Hello, Johnson!" Dr.David laughed, and walked toward him.

"My friend, please sit down."Johnson gestured to him. Johnson grinned as he watched Dr.David slowly take a chair. Professor Johnson looked in his eye and found his friend obviously agitated and on tenterhooks.

"David, what's up? Tell me what troubles you?" He asked.

Dr.David closed his eyes for a moment and recollected with a sense of injury. He felt rather ashamed to disclose it before his friend, although the thought itself filled him an overwhelming misery, compounded by a feeling of fright. After a moment's pause, he cleared his throat and explained everything in a voice trembled with emotion. His tone was far more convincing than the words he said. In few words he told the whole story about his illicit relationship with Miss. Ann. He choked back when he told about her betrayal and her ruthless streak of cruelty in her.

Dr. David was on the verge of a cry. He was at an utter loss and enfeebled morally and physically. He admitted that he couldn't bear her betrayal and understand the cruel, merciless logic of Miss. Ann.

Professor Johnson grew pensive. The thought of a frivolous, stupid young woman suddenly turned out as a sneak thief and disappearing after looting a huge sum from his doctor friend really flabbergasted him.

"Good heavens! It's really cruel and inhuman. This is an enormous crime. Why don't you lodge a complaint in the police station?" he asked, knitting his brow and rubbing his forehead.

Dr.David took a deep breath."Well, you know, I am rather afraid about my daughter. What will I do if she ever finds out my illicit connection with Miss.Ann? I don't want her to know about it, and the police men interrogating her about the robbery...."

Professor Johnson seemed touched to the heart and he began to talk incessantly. He even asked some fatuous questions in a curious manner. Dr. David responded listlessly and even forced a smile at his friend's witticism. After a moment's pause, Johnson began to talk in a roundabout way about the cruel, selfish women in general who commit crime abnormally.

Dr. David listened in complete silence, his eyes filled with tears. When the steward brought them the drinks, he took the glass and drank at a draught with a melancholy face.

Finally, Johnson consoled his friend and suddenly got to his feet. Listening to the uproar and loud talk mingled with laughter in the club room, he said.

"Let's walk a bit of the way. I am tired of sitting."

When they had walked out of the club, it was dark outside and a light mist was drifting over the grass.

Dr. David suddenly returned back from the reverie and glanced around his lobby. With a deep sigh, he again sank back in his chair, resting his head against the cushion. He looked at the wall clock. It was half past eight. He had to go for the rounds. He looked about uneasily at him, with a sinking feeling. A kind of uncontrollable self loathing had him its grip.

"Well, I can't drop the theft for the moment when she bullies me again. I have to make a decision before I fall in to a drunken stupor for days on end." He thought hard, raking his mind.

"Yes, I must call Mr. Johnson and inform him about her bully. I can wait for his final say. He's such a nice man and a generously kind hearted human being..."

Dr. David made up his mind, picked up the receiver, and dialed the number. Seconds later, Johnson's warm voice was heard over the line. From the absurdity of his position and dilemma, Dr.David burst in to a hysterical laughter and began to talk about the bully.

"Hello, David, I assure you this would not go in to such a problem. Don't worry! We will handle this bully together. I swear, I will find a way to get you out of this imbroglio. You just relax and make yourself comfortable..." Johnson said soothingly, struggling not to laugh. The conversation went about five minutes.

Finally, Dr. David heaved a sigh of relief and replaced the receiver. Then mopping his brow, he sat down heavily behind his table with a broad grin on his face.

A few days later, on a fine evening, Dr.David went out his house and strode towards the nearby river. Across the river the sky was flooded with red. The sun was setting. The broad river and the square vegetable plot on the bank were flooded with purple light. He could see flocks of pigeons, gilded by the setting sun, wheeling over the vegetable garden.

Dr. David was sorely troubled and restless. He walked down the vegetable garden, glancing now and again at the village women tearing off cabbage leaves and talking in loud voices. Beyond the vegetable garden, there was a row of thick clumps of bushes leaning over the water. The setting sun was reflected near the left bank. Small rippling waves ran over its reflection. The river bank was stretched out with dark shapes of several cottages loomed behind the slender trunks of riverside trees.

When he came to the river, there was an urgent need in his mind. He was expecting to meet the laundress at the bathing hut. Walking round the bathing hut, he saw large bath towels and dresses left drying on the railing of the little bridge. He stepped on to the bridge and stood there for a moment, idly fingering a bath towel, which was rough and cold to touch. Then he kept looking round and decided to wait until he could meet the laundress at there.

The river flowed quickly and gurgled around the piles supporting the bathing hut. For some time, he forgot the world and peered at the river glimmering at the distance. Aimless and vague thoughts kept pestering and drag one after another in his head. He remembered how fate, in the person of that strange woman, had caressed him by mistake, gradually making him a sinner. It seemed as a senseless joke and he began to spite the fate.

"How stupid is my life!"He thought, gazing at the fast flowing river. "My life is mad, restless and troubled, like the river in a rainy season. And My heart is so heavy, like the heavy sediment lies on the bottom of the river..."

Dr. David hung about a while at the bridge and as he couldn't meet the laundress, he eventually decided to go back. He walked back with long strides hardly noticing anything around him.

When he came back after his evening stroll, it was dark and everything around his house was merged in to a solid blackness. The alley in front of his house was also dark and deserted. He reached his house tired and sank heavily in to a chair by the front door to take rest. He looked in to his watch. It was exactly seven 'o clock. A bit of the moon was peeped out behind the clouds.

He groped in one pocket to pull out his cigarettes and silently gazed at the moon hung high above the garden. The whole world seemed to be made up of black silhouettes and wandering white shadows in the drifting mist. He tapped out a Wills and slowly lit it. While dragging the cigarette, he unintentionally planted his legs wide apart. Suddenly his left foot brushed against something soft. Dr.David curiously glanced at the side of his left foot and suddenly gave a start. He uttered a rasping cry and as if with horror,that ghastly contorted his face.

What he saw was a bundle lay under the very front door, wrapped as an oblong object. One end of the bundle was slightly open. Terrified he sprang to his feet and threw the smoldering cigarette away. Abruptly he knelt down, thrust his hand in the opening and felt something warm and moist.

"Oh, my Lord! She has disgraced me for life! She has left it at my door step!" He rose to his feet, fisted his hands and hissed through his clenched teeth.

"Ah! There it lies before me! I remember her despicable conversation, importunate enough, in which she blamed me harshly....The wages of sin!"

He stood as if stunned by fear, resentment and shame.

"What would I do? What would my daughter say if she found out? The whole hill station would know my secret, and most likely, the respectable people would forbid me to their house. All the news papers and T.V.Channels would flash about the foundling, and..and.. My humble name would be bandied everywhere..."

He turned toward the left side of the porch, leaning against the wall. The dining room window was open and he could clearly hear his daughter giving instructions to the maid in a husky whisper while she laid the table for supper.

Dr. David glanced fearfully at his daughter and twitched his small beard like a magpie its tail.

"If the baby awakened and cried, the secret would be out!"He felt an irresistible urge to run.

"Hurry, *hurry,* "he muttered to himself, "Not time to waste. Go as fast as you can. Go while the going is good. I have to take him somewhere and leave him on someone else's porch."

Dr.David picked up the bundle with both hands and started down the street at a steady, measured step so as not to arouse suspicion.

"What a horrid situation!"He said to himself, trying to maintain a casual air.

"A renowned Doctor, worried and walking down the street with a baby in his arms! O Lord, if someone sees me and guesses the truth, I am finished!"

While walking he could see the narrow road meandered upward in the bright light of the moon and shining stars. The long line of trees on either side of the road was merged in to darkness. Here and there and far away, dim lights were burning in the cottages. To the left of the road, a hill covered with low shrubs, giving it a curly look, ran parallel to the road. A large moon, slightly filmed with mist and surrounded by little, ragged clouds, hung high above the hill motionlessly as if witnessing his wickedness.

"Where could I take him? I know, I will take him to Professor Johnson's place. He's my bosom friend, married for years and childless. He's rich and compassionate too, and he may be grateful for the baby. He will surely bring him up as a son."

Dr. David's mind was made up.

Yes, professor Johnson it was to be, even though his Villa is at the far end of the road, right on the river bank.

"If only the baby doesn't start bawling and slip out of this blanket."

Dr.David began to collect the images of his friend and wife flickering in his imagination in to a single whole, with a pleasant surprise on their faces.

"Now, supposing his family adopts the baby, I should not be surprised if he went way up in the world. He might become a professor or something, an engineer or a writer… Everything is possible in the world! Look at me! Here I am carrying him in my arms like so much rubbish, and twenty or twenty five from now on, perhaps I will have to stand before him with respect and admiration…"

As Dr.David hurried along the narrow deserted lanes past long fences in the dark, black shadows cast by the line of trees, suddenly a thought stabbed him that he was doing something very cruel and criminal.

"It's the vilest thing anyone could do. He's my flesh and blood and what am I doing? I am going to toss this poor infant at my friend's porch mercilessly. How's the baby to blame? Scoundrel that I am! I have also a doubt whether the baby has life of misery in store… Here I am taking him to Johnson's place, hoping he's benevolent. What if he will put him in an orphanage to live among some incorrigible, shabby little strangers? Everything is impersonal there, with no one to fondle, love or pamper him…And then… afterwards he will be apprenticed to some sort of a mechanic or work men living in a shanty, to learn work the hard way. My son will start drinking, use foul language, will live from hand to mouth. A mechanic apprentice indeed, when he's the son of a renowned doctor, a man of noble blood!.."

Dr. David broke in to a sob as he entered from the shadow of trees in to the brightly lit pathway. He slowly un-wrapped the bundle and took a look at the baby.

"Ah, my son is sleeping! Look at him! How beautiful he is..!"

After trudging up a little he came to Johnson's villa.While climbing the stairs stealthily,his conscience pricked at his heart.Carefully he laid the bundle down near the doorstep.His mind was thronged with many problems. Then he turned to go with a hopeles gesture.Suddenly he felt tears crawling down his cheeks again.

"Forgive me babe,villain that I am!" Then he held his breath and tip toed out in to the darkness. He walked along the river bank with profound grief. He could sense the still, deep slumber of the river. There was not a scrap of shade on the moon lit weir. Only the meloncholy, monotonous chirping of the crickets and the distant call of a quail were disrupting the nocturnal silence.

At seven o' clock in the morning, professor Johnson was awakened out of a deep sleep by his wife's loud call.He got out of bed,fighting the exhaustion. Rubbing sleep from his eyes,he stared at Nancy. She was holding carefully an oblong object wrapped up in a small quilt. Nancy walked over to him,looking at his puzzled face.

"What's it?" He asked,stiffling a yawn.

"Look here! A baby! somebody has left it at the door step.."

Carefully,she laid the bundle on the bed.Johnson could hear the baby breath hard and fast.

"Ah, an abandoned baby!" Johnson exclaimed with a tinge of gloom in his phlegmatic voice. Nancy had a small feeding bottle in her hand. She slowly thrusted the nipple between the baby's pale mouth.

"There, suck the milk baby!" She smiled when the baby's mouth twitched and sneezed.She watched the baby drinking greedily and she hummed a song emotionally.After a short while the baby fell asleep.

"He's sleeping,"Nancy whispered,"look at him,he's got his daddy's hooked nose,the scamp!"

"What do you mean,Nancy?" Johnson blurted out as if stunned by fear and shame.

"Ah! Are you shrinking from fear and shame?" She retorted with a derisive look.

"Nancy! what are you imagining?" Johnson cried with a flushed face.

"Tell me,Johnson,is it our former parlour made,Stella?"

"You mean, the baby's mother? I don't know.."Johnson mumbled incoherently.

Nancy creased her brow in suspicion and continued.

"Here me out! This is your child. You have sinned! Now I can understand everything. I remember your relationship with Stella. I am damn sure it's your momentary aberration and she got pregnant….."

Johnson cried again and fell on his knees before her.

"Nancy, what are you cooking up?"

"Well, I am not indicting on charges ranging from arson to murder. I am telling the truth. He's your son…" Nancy said taking a deep breath of anger and watched Johnson's face as if to find a small frission of guilt. With a wave of hands he got on his feet and dashed out of the room like a whipped dog ran outside. Nancy watched his flight and she couldnot help smiling.

Johnson ran out side of his house with a hopeless gesture." OH, my God! How can she imagine it! Is my wife simply a fancy stuff!..."

He suddenly felt a lump in his throat and he began to cough with never a pause. It was a kind of wailing,wheezy cough. He walked swiftly across the green lawn and toward the gate.

"How stupid I am! Why didn't I protest?" He thought gazing at a young woman standing out side the gate.She had a perplexed look on her face.

Watching Johnson for a moment,she shrugged and walked past the gate.A minute later she came back and opened the gate.Then she went straight to him and again shrugged her shoulders.

"Sir, I am.. I am Rita the laundress. The news paper boy told me that sombody has left my baby here on the veranda…" She mumbled in a feeble voice.

"What? what did you say?" Johnson shouted at the top of his voice.The laundress scratched her head in embarrassment and heaved a sigh. Glancing up she met Johnson's astonished,pop-eyed glare.

The laundress mumbled apologetically.

"Sir, it's my fault to leave my baby at Doctor David's veranda yesterday. Leaving my baby at there, I went to see his neighbour with my thickly wrapped cloth bundle. When I came back a short while later,my baby was not there. I called the doctor. His daughter said that he was out somewhere and she didn't know any thing about the baby. I could only search every where in fright.I guess that Doctor David brought my child here out of confusion. I am so sorry…."

Johnson listened dumbly,his mouth gaped and disbelief on his face.The laundress followed Johnson as he stormed toward the house.

"What the hell you have done to me!" He roared, "Don't you even know how panicky I am! My heart is aching. I don't know whether it's a heart burn or a heart attack!" He turned to the laundress in the hall as she waddled past him hurriedly. Johnson waited out side and listened the laundress conversing loudly with Nancy inside the bed room.

"So!", he exclaimed," Doctor David, you thought it's your child! You supposed on reasonable ground that Ann had laid the baby at your door step… You idiot!"

A silence ensued in the bed room.When Johnson eagerly came inside the bedroom,he could see the astonished face of Nancy.The laundress nodded to him and went out side carrying the baby carefully with her hands.

"My darling! My darling!" She mumbled as she walked out,her pale face twisted in a smile.

"What a nice kettle of fish,I tell you!" Johnson muttered with a wide grin.

"A hell of a business!"

Nancy heaved a loud sigh, "My God, a comfort for some minutes have gone!"

She looked sadly at Johnson standing at the door post with an undefinable elation.Suddenly he burst in to a loud laughter.

"Nancy, now I have no confession to make. But still the joke is on me!" He went over and took Nancy's hand in his.

CHAPTER 5

ONE OF LIFE'S TRIVIA

It was just after half past ten.Dry leaves,which fell from the towering eyucalyptus trees flanked by the road,surled in the wind and fell over a bronze monument in front of the hospital building.

Doctor David was unable to shake the feeling of depression that hung over him.He was sitting in his office,resting his hands on the desk.He remembered his morning round that went bad. The first stop was a ward containing a dozen patients.Hurriedly he went to the first patient and looked at the chart at the foot of the bed.

He raised his head slowly and said to the patient, "You need a bronchoscopy test this morning…"

The patient nodded and coughed badly.

"Did you take the medicine?" Doctor David frowned.

"Yes, Doc,all of the capsules you gave me yesterday …"The fat –bellied patient said between his fits of cough and moved ungainly on the bed.

"Well, you have to take Ampicillin four times a day.."

Doctor David said as he moved to him and drawing a handful of Ampicillin capsules out of his coat pocket. Doctor david was entirely unusuall from his colleauges with his curious customs and intimacy to his patients.He looked down, turned the capsules over his right hand and took one by the other.He looked at it, rubbed it between his fingers and began to talk seriously about his patient's case history. Finally,he turned and walked toward the other patient on the next bed. Before talking to his next patient he swallowed the tablet.

"That's not right, Doc! You forget to give me the capsule…and you swallowed it!"

Doctor David turned to the first patient with a queer look.

"Ah,you are right! I am not supposed to take your medicine four times a day..i am sorry!" Suddenly the capsules in his right fist slipped through his fingers and fell on the floor.

"Ah, what's happening to me? My mind is constantly carried away by something.." He muttered to one of the nurses who bent down and picked the tablet one by one. Then She walked over to the first patient who was bursting in to a loud laughter. Dr. David watched him,scratching his head.

"Smething beats the hell out of me!" Suddenly he began to sweat and he felt colics in his stomach. The blood in his head went boom, boom! He went hot and cold from the thought that he's unwell and went crazy. He turned round the nurses gathered round him and said hoarsely,spacing out the syllable.

"I am sorry. I cannot come with you for the rounds. I am not feeling well..." He started waving off a supervising nurse and walked past them toward the door.Groping for the door handle,and before stepping out,he muttered irritably.

"Ah, nobody understands my personal grief!"

The silence dragged and slowly he roused from his recollection. He stroked his sideburns,thinking about his bad state of affairs. He was worried about the conjectural matters being gossipped between the hospital staff. He had already overheard some nasty conversations about his absent mindedness and strange demeanor.He was also shocked and worried greatly. Somany times he had seen many furtive glances at his face by his colleagues gathered in the corridor.

Doctor David heaved a sigh and looked out through the large glass window.

The distant hills were flooded with bright sunlight.The air was clear and a dampness seemed to be spreading through it. The mist whirling round the ravines was dissolved with a blaze covering half the sky.

Slowly Doctor David picked up the receiver and dialed.

"Ah, I am agonized. I still have that little whore black mailing me from the valley.."

Doctor David uttered a sickly laugh while he attended the phone.

"Hello, Johnson. I am too scared to say my friend. You know, it's very queer and amazing for you..!"

"Good morning Doctor,"he heard Johnson's surprised voice on the line.

"Tell me everything that bother you...."

Doctor David passed a trembling hand over his fore head,took a deep breath and began to explain.

"My friend!" He cried and his voice trailed in to a fit of sobbing.

"Miss. Ann has brought her baby yesterday and abandoned him at my doorstep.You know, Johnson, how much I took fright. I was agonized and afraid of the public opinion to bring up the baby at my home. I was in a state of confusion. So, I wrapped up the baby and secretly left him yesterday evening on your veranda. Forgive me for my impudence. Now, I humbly beseech you to adopt him.And then my son would always happy with you. I pray,don't wreck the life of my innocent babe. I will hand over you a wad of cash,a huge amount… please do help me!"

Every sincere intentions to save the baby had at last burst out of his heart in to the open. He paused for a moment and felt his mouth parched. He also felt unbearably miserable and he had an irresistible urge for a drink.

There was silence for a moment.Then he heard Johnson's nervous voice again on the phone.

"Mr. David, did your daughter tell anything about Rita, the laundress?"

"Rita? No, not at all! why do you talk about her?"

"Well, friend you have nothing to worry about the baby. Because the baby you abandoned at my doorstep is Rita's. And now she had brought the missing baby back.It's not Miss. Ann's babe, after all.."

"What? Are you kidding?" The news was surprisingly heavy for Doctor David.He heard Johnson's loud wheezy snicker on the line.

"It's true,my friend. And tell me whether did you get any call from Miss. Ann today?"

"No, she didn't call me so far." Doctor David blinked his eyes as he heard Johnson's long peels of laughter. Suppressing his laughter, Johnson explained a plan.

"Okay, David,then let us arrange a surprise visit at her house. Let us go to the valley this afternoon itself. Within an hour I would reach out you. Let us go together as visitors,sothat we could change the vengeful thoughts on her mind."

"Well, Johnson, it would be good to reach out her before she storm out here and make a fuss around.come on now…"

Doctor David put the reciever back and nervously chewed on his moustache.

For some hours of tedious driving brought them off the main road down the valley to a gravelly grit road,and driving became bumpy.After a few minutes driving,during which they were disturbed by a large herd of sheeps,the driving became worse. Sliding the down hill,they saw a sparkling river with it's skirting,captivating length. Streams of afternoon light flowed all along the sliding road,and by the far and wide meadows. Finally, they came before a large green field with long fences trailing out along the peasant cottages,huddled against each other.

Doctor David and Johnson clumsily got out of the car and walked toward the cottage's direction. Dr. David was in an unsteady gait and he burped. His hang over and drowsiness left him in a trice. As they walked, they could see an old peasant sitting on the ground and trimming off green branches with a small axe. Johnson stopped before him and chatted with the peasant. Within a short while, he gathered required information about Miss. Ann and her uncle. On the way to Miss. Ann's cottage,they had to walk past a large garden of all concievable local and foreign fruit trees.

Finally, they arrived at Miss. Ann's cottage,huddled between pines on a tiny,square plot. As they crossed the fence, both of them started by the shrill barking of a hound of very dark colour. Fortunately enough for them,the dog was in chain and tethered to an iron post. Near the cottage, they were met by a boy of eight years old,with freckles on his astonished face. He looked at the stranger for a moment in silence,his eyes bulging, then probably he could not recognize them,he gasped and ran head long in to the cottage.

"I know why did he run…" laughed Johnson with a wink.

"He might be recoiled at the thought that one of us is a suiter who came to court Miss. Ann!"

"May be! Johnson,you can prefer yourself as the suiter…" Doctor David remarked,bursting in to laughter, "Ha, ha! A cow girl for my professor!"

Johnson expressed his resentment, "Doctor, you forget your liaison with Miss. Ann. You would be a better suiter for her…."

"Alas! How can I prefer myself for her suiter? Once, she had stolen a huge amount, and all I can openly call her now is a thief. But,let us drop the theft for the moment.It's better to stop her tantrums as a black mailer…."

Doctor David blurted out as they climbed the stairs. Johnson knocked on the closed door and waited. Nobody answered. They fell silent and turned pensive. A minute later,they heard footsteps behind the door. A lock clicked on the door and infront of them, they saw an enquiring expression on the face of an old man.

"Hello, uncle! Is Miss. Ann at home?" Johnson asked curiously.

"She's not here. She went to the town this morning..." Replied the old man,slightly shivering at the damp air that blew in on him.

They went in to the drawing room following the doddering old man. Soft, strange sounds of children were borne round the rooms.

In the drawing room,two crumpled cushions lay on one of the settes upholstered in pale-blue silk. Up on a round table infront of the sette,they noticed a bottle of whisky and a glass with few drops in it.

The old man glanced obliquely at his visitors with a face of aversion. Johnson gathered from his face that he had reasons for his rudeness. Johnson was the first to speak.

"Allow me to introduce first,"He said sitting heavily on the sette," I am professor Johnson.And let me introduce my friend Doctor David...."

"Doctor David!" The old man exclaimed,looking gravely and inquiringly at the Doctor.

"Yes. Please excuse us for breaking in to your little cottage.We want to meet your Niece, Ann mary.." Doctor David said as he sat next to Johnson. He lit a cigarette and dragged on it.

"We want to have time to talk Ann Mary before we go back.When will she return from the town?"

"I don't know,sir.May be she would come after fiv o' clock."The old man mumbled in a broken voice. The visitors asked some questions and made his acquaintance. The old man sat respectfully on a high backed chair by the window and talked. A little later, he rose up and muttered,while slowly walking toward the round table.

"Sir, we are simple folks.Not such respectable people like both of you. We won't believe in showing off..No sir... Shall I serve tea for you?"

Johnson declined with a courteous smile.

"Then would you let me take another glass, please!" He asked as if it's not proper to drink in the presence of strangers before he got their permission. The oldman man poured whisky in to the glass. He took the glass,looking askance at the visitors, and silently drained it, as if he does not want to hurt the feelings of the visitors.

"Sir, I know what you are thinking right now!" He said,becoming drunkenly and habitually inflamed by the whisky.

"You are thinking that I have gone to pot,that I am sunk and so senile. You suspect that I have lost my health out of dissipation. May be my health is deteriorating,but I am happy sir. To my mind this simple life is much more happy and normal than your opulant way of life. I don't need anybody's help.. I don't even intend to grovel at the feet of the rich, though I am out of work. My children look after me......"

Then,with an unsteady gait, he shuffled his way to the kitchen.

"And here is my kitchen..", he said,bending a little as he entered the small-ceilinged room which was unbearably stuffy.

His wife and grand children were sitting at a table,eating and drinking. Johnson got up and walked toward the kitchen door. The appearance of the stranger made them exchange surprised looks and stop them chewing.

"Come on,sir! Will you call the doctor too?Take a seat,be so kind. We don't stand on ceremony.We live simply, sir..." Mumbled the old man. He leaned forward and took a bottle from the table.

"Ah,I will take another glass of whisky on account of this pickled mushroom!"

He smacked his lips. Happily, he glanced over his shoulder at the door, and saw Johnson walking back.

Johnson sat again on the sette and took out a cigarette out of his packet. He struck one match after another and lit the cigarette. He was thinking humourously about the oldman's drunker stupour and his behaviour in his inebriate condition.

"Mr. David, a nasty lot are these drunkards. Every day they chase after each and every tavern shamelessly....." He beamed with an inanely wide smile at David.

'I don't think so. Actually, the drunkards are taking up a space in the world, delighted more than us. Comparing to them, what good are we? A nasty lot of hard working intelligentsia obsessed with moral principles!" Doctor David laughed.

The old man came toward them,holding the neck of the mushroom pickle bottle in his right hand,and two empty glasses on the other. He put them all on the round table with a drunken smirk. He was considerably intoxicated after two or three glasses he had,and he was feeling maudlin. He seemed that he could not resist an urge to his new sensations about his family and he began to blab out his feelings to both of them.

"You know,sir,my son in law, a very nice looking gentle man, was head over heels in love with my daughter. He was rich and belonged to an aristocratic family. H e married my daughter,loved his wife and had children. After his love affair ended in matriomony,and after his first child born,he went to abroad. He's now working in Dubai…."

"Well, a nice gentleman! It's a true successful love story,indeed. What's your daughter's name?"

Doctor David asked interestingly as the old man hung his head in thoughts. The tall,sineway old man,balded and with a grey beard seemed to him pondering over something. Suddenly, he looked up and muttered.

"Well, sir, my daughter's name is Natasha. It may seem a strange name to both of you. She's pretty and intelligent. She's an actress in a professional drama troop. Last night she went for a benefit performance.She 's a lot of admirers who storm in to her dressing room,just to appreciate her talent. It's a pleasure to say that,recently she got an offer to act in a Tamil TV.Serial. She earns a lot…" He paused and remained silent for a minute.Then he burst in to laughter,a kind of drunken,coughing laughter.

"Mm,old age! I am old and weak. I have already got one foot in the grave! what shall I do? I still depend on my children…." He mumbled as if in a delirium.

Johnson listened tensely,staring at the oldman with unblinking eyes. Suddenly the old man called his wife,loudly stamping his right foot on the floor.

"Maria, bring me a tumbler filled with cold water.."

A moment later, his wife, Maria came in with a child,and after settling the boy on the sofa in a corner,she went in to the kitchen. Very soon she returned with a tumbler of water and put it on the round table. She smiled to the visitors and waddled back to the child. The boy moved uneasily on the sofa,his eyes screwed up and puffing.

"Do stay,child." She said and went in to the kitchen.The old man moved closely to the visitors.

"Sir, if you don't mind, let me propose a toast to. My throat is terribly dry!" He drew the chair to the table and sat on the brink of it. Johnson watched him pour out in three glasses and cautiously add cold water up to the brim of the glasses. Dr. David and Johnson smiled and exchanged glances. They silently took their glasses and proposed a toast. The old man crossed a sign himself, took his glass and drank up at a draught. He placed the glass down and took the bulging bottle of mushroom pickle with his both hands. He watched his guests with a rapturous smile and poured a bit of mush room pickle on his right palm. He began to lick the pickle with relish as he found his guests were in a good,exuberent mood. He looked happily on their faces as if he had found his guests were got in to the swing of their role as drunkards. He was really happy. As for him, the presence of sobermen act irritatingly on drunken mechanism!

"Sir, whisky is a terrible stuff. It outright brings up intoxication and leave us pretty soon,as if passing out intoxication unnoticed...." The oldman mumbled, looking at the half drained bottle of whisky with evident revulsion.

Maria came again,bringing a plate of porridge and a spoon. She placed them on Teapoy infront of the child. "Eat,baby." She told him.

Johnson looked at the baby. He was an infant of three with a sorrowful look. His face was small,thin, freckled,pointed at the chin like a squirrel's.His great black eyes were shining with liquid brilliance.

"It's Natasha's seccond child." The old man introduced the child,as he dropped his head despondently. It seemed that he is not used to eat by himself.

The oldman simply shook his head with a compassionate look at the child.

"Ah, my baby is so pampered up! Look at his curly hair and bright eyes! You know, sir, when he smiles,his smile alone reminds me that perpetual half-merry,half absent smile of Jacob...."

"So, I presume that Jacob is Natasha's husband,am I right?"

Doctor David asked,looking at the child with a delighted smile.

"No,sir, you are not right. Jacob is an actor in Natasha's drama troop. He's a slender,graceful youngman from a respectable family..." The old man chuckled.

"I am sorry it came out like that and I asked about Jacob!"

Doctor David mumbled with a perplexed look,and digging his left eye with his index finger.

"Well, Doctor, the old man nis letting the cat out of his bag in his inebriate condition! A good family, indeed!" Johnson murmured, glaring at the Doctor in amazement.

Suddenly, they heard hurried footsteps outside,followed by a humming tune,and within a moment Ann mary appeard at the door.A nice looking gentleman,about twenty five years old,went along with her,clumsily put his arm around her waist. They stepped over the threshold,talking something in subdued voices. Both of them suddenly stood stock still in the drawing room,looking at the visitors.They exchanged glancess,and whispered something inarticulately together.Ann mary released herself with an effort,and strided to ward Doctor David with a pale face.

"Hello,Doctor,I couldn't believe my eyes,truly! What a surprise!"

Ann mary not only rolled her eyes in amazement,but fluttered her hands.

Doctor David's heart was pounding.He shifted his legs and straightened himself out. Doctor David drew a deep breath and glanced up and down her.

Miss. Ann was dressed very provocatively,wearing a tight low-cut mini dress with high heels that showed off her slender legs.The crimson halter top had beneath it a push up bra that showed off her cleavage.The dress clung every curve of her body,classy and sexy. Dr. David had a flight of imagination. He imagined his mouth on her tits,sucking them and her luscious body feeling warm and tingly while he played with her boobs.

"pull yourself Ann!."

The nice looking gentleman mumbled and gave a nudge on her elbows. Ann mary turned her pallid face to him and tried a smile.Her hands were shaking as if cold waves were running up and down all her insides.

"Nice to meet you, Ann." Doctor David said,moping his brow," And tell me who is this Gentle man?"

Ann mary swallowed hard "He is.. he's Mr. Nelson, my fiance..." Her voice was tremulous.

Mr. Nelson moved forward and smiled at Doctor David.He said nothing as if he tried to be as quite as possible.

"Nice! You got a good selection." Doctor said as if impressed. Yet his smal,bloated eyes looked out sullenly from under his brows at Mr. Nelson. He seemed recoiled from Doctor's stare,but he was calm and his red fleshy face wore an indifferent expression.

Nleson moved closely,proffered his hand to the doctor and muttered, "I am so glad to meet you,Doctor." Doctor grinned and shook hands with him.

Nelsn turned to Ann mary and muttered, backing away a step.

"I am leaving Ann. Let's see tomorrow." He went back with a drooping head and stepped out of the room. Ann took a deep breath.

"I am sorry,Doctor, for all that came out like this! I want to talk something personal to you.come with me please! let's talk inside my bedroom."She spoke in jerky sentences,like a frightened,and shocked maid. She looked askance at Johnson. He was dragging a cigarette,and beaming all the while with a mischievious look.

Ann mary boldly walked over to Doctor David,groped for his hand,while tossing her head to Johnson.

'I am sorry, professor. I have to talk to him seriously…"

Johnson looked at her uncle. The oldman was pretending a sleep after his drunken bouts. He was sitting at a high back chair by the window.His eyes were closed,his head hung and snorring.while snoring he mumbled in coherently.

"Ah! She has come at a worse time!"

Doctor David was obviously undecided what to do.

"Look,Doctor. I can understand your emotions.come with me. let's talk together". Ann mary spoke hotly,cluthing at his shirt sleeve. Doctor David exchanged glances with Johnson. He nodded. Doctor David got on his feet and followed Ann Mry toward her bed room.

"At last!", Ann Mary sighed with relief,groping for the door handle, "As God is my witness, I feel relieved. Come in,sir. let's talk…"

She went in a crampy little room and switched on the ceiling fan. Doctor David closed the door and walked behind Ann,his hands thrust in his trouser pockets. He inclined his head to oneside and gazed at Ann closely.Looking at her body in motion made him feel unexpectedly aroused. The movement of her hips,her flexing buttocks in her tight low-cut mini dress and the slight bounce of her breasts as she walked enticed him. His rage was somewhat hitched up. Ann mary blinked her eyes rapidly,sat down at a table and pointed a chair next to her with a pixie smile. She watched his flushed face. And only by the tiny drops glistening in his cheeks that she could believe he was crying silently. There was a subtle,barely perceptible grief on his tearstained face. Doctor David sat next to her,controlling his emotion. He straightened the fringed shade of an unlit lamp and glanced in to a thick book lying on the table.

"Sir, I gues that you have not forgotten me."

Her voice was trembled with emotion. Licking her red lips, she placed her hand on his thigh and slowly moved it up his fly under the table cloth. Doctor David gave a start and grunted. "you better careful with your hand of yours..."

She took her hand and reached for a cigarette pack on the table. She picked up one and offered Doctor David the cigarette. He took it and placed it between his lips with a sarcastic smile. She held the lighter up and lit the cigarette.

"Thank you." He said,letting the smoke lightly drift from his lips.

"Ann you different now. You are something else!" he said in a whisper.

She nodded. "Yes, doctor.I am not a good girl." She said lowering her voice.

"What are you doing now?" He asked curiously.

"I run a fancy shop in the town selling a lot of cosmetics,perfumes and fancy jwelleries. I made it possible by spending your money on it. And let me tell somethiing about my fiance,Nelson. He's a nice, intelligent guy.He owns a grocery store adjacent to my shop.He offered to help me start my shop closeby. You know, he's a simpleton and he told me that he did never had affairs with women. Oneday, much to my surprise, he fell on his knees before me and told that he's in love with me! And pretty well soon, we fell in love..."

Ann looked up Doctor David's eyes with perceptible guilt. There was a surge of emotion in his eyes.

"I am sorry Doctor, I was cloyingly insincere to you. I have stolen your wad of cash and precious ornaments. I admit, I was so tactless,so crass and stupid! Forgive me! In the past,I was so defenceless and poor,dependent on the rich and noble. So, oneday I want to live indipendent,even by involving in somekind of dreadful buisiness. And I had to do a horrible thing to you by thieiving and running away. I didn't foresee how cruel it was,. I couldn't foresee your sense of injury compounded by a feeling of revulsion and disgust against me. It was so unfair and cruel on my part......"

Doctor David stroked his sideburns and said emotionally.

"Ann,I am very glad to hear your confession. In the past, I always considerd you as an innocent lamb. But oneday you shocked me with betrayal and infidility,wrecking my life in to loneliness. You know, I am not bothered about the theft,but your foul play and I could hardly stand it for months. You did dare to make sport of my honour by way of a despicable and vile play. You made me a useless stage prop out of my ridiculous infatuation. I admit, it's also my fault! You know, I had been fallen out since you left me. My innocent daughter found me under a spell of diissipation and sullen rancour. She herself couldn't understand why I suddenly changed and began to hate her. And she feared every step I made toward her......."

"I am sorry Doctor, but I can't find an answer." Ann whispered in a quivering voice. Tears were glistening on her lashes. She dropped her head and pulled at her leather bag. She took out a folded kerchief and dabbed at her eyes.

"Do forgive me!," She mumbled, "I have so much respect for you that my heart aches!"

"Don't cry, Ann. I am forgetting every thing. Past is past." Doctor David wrinkled his brow in puzzlement.

"Ann, I forgive you although you fucked me hard! You know, time flew,which meant that life's good and easy for both of us...'Doctor David paused, as he felt more awkward at her sobs and he went completely at a loss for words.

"Come now,come,baby!", He mumbled, "Why cry really? I didn't intend to hurt your feelings!"

"What's the matter with me?," Doctor David thought aghast, "I do love her still..or do I!'"

Ann Mary recovered, stopped crying,and already she was breathing easily and lightly.

"Doctor, I can't stand this terrible situation. You know, I still love you! But, I am going to be betrothed. It's terrible!" She whispered with a look of acute pain on her face.

Doctor David took a deep breath and squashed out his cigarette in an ashtray.

"Ann, I have got to say nothing to you particulary. I am happy that you still love me. But,you have to get married with Nelson. After all, I can afford to stand your jilt!" He burst in to a jolly laughter.

"But,Ann,let me ask you a final question. Why did you contrive a plan to black mail me? After that I really felt injured and gone crazy..."

Ann Mary completely recovered herself and began looking at his eyes pleadingly.

"Sir, I promise that I will not dare to go down for anything. Not for anything in the world,I swear. Let me reveal that it was not actually my plan. I didn't either want to bully or blackmail you. It was my aunt, Natasha's plan. She often drove me frantic with an urge to plunder you. She knew all the relationship between you and me. She made me mad,selfish and spiteful again. She had a plan to buy off an expensive aparment in town,so that we could all settle on there. She urged me to pick up extramoney and compelled to call you. That's why I blackmailed you to stash a huge amount in my Axis bank account. Natasha organised the game so tactfully. She was greedy and crazy of money.. I beg your pardon….."

"it's okay, Ann. I pardon you, and I don't want to make any trouble to you." Doctor David laughed as if relaxed.

Ann Mary looked at his eyes thankfully. She smiled coquettishly as if a flower blossoming in the sunlight. She bravely put her arms around Doctor David's shoulders and drew him closer to her.

"Thank you,Doctor. Thank you very much!" She mumbled as she snuggled up to him and kissed on his cheek.Suddenly her hand went down for his fly,and then befor the Doctor could knew it,she began to feel the hard on growing against the touch of her hand. She smiled at him bewitchingly and whimpered.

"I guess that you have'nt gotten off in a long time …" And before he knew it,she opened his fly.

"Sir, let me please do it. for the last time, just to rub my thumb over the tip of your…" She stopped in mid –sentence and gasped out.

"Please Doctor,please let me do it. I know you like it very much! Ah! Why are you taking my hand away?.."

Doctor David was so excited and enraged that he he scrambled his English in jerky sentences.

"Hell! What's this? Tell me what are you up to? You are putting me in to an awfully ticklish position!"

"Well, Doctor, I don't want to fuck you right now. I just wanted to feel you and share my emotions. I missed you so far,honey!" Ann said.

With lowered lids,and breathing a hot stream of air,she brought her face close to him.Her wet mouth opened and her tongue moved slowly against his lips. She touched his face with her shaking fingers,tracing the line of his jaw and the soft spot on his neck where his pulse hammered a message of desire.

Doctor david was momentarily shocked and paralysed. He couldn't hold her,and slowly he responded to her kiss. He heard a new melody that had always been in the back of his mind. Miss. Ann breathed hard and fast,framed his face with her hands and moved her head, deepening her kiss.

Controlling for his breath, Doctor David shook his head.

"Stop! No!"

"What's happened?" She asked quikly,with an echo of dissappointment lacing her voice.

Why? why had he ruined it? she was falling for him frantically. The man she had known for months reeling with sexual vertigo in his dim lit bedroom!

Ann mary could feel him slipping away and evidently scarring her completely. Her final resolve to make him under the spell of love and passion had crumbled.

Stroking her dark hair that spanned around her shoulders,she tried to smile meekly with an unmasked dissappointment in her eyes.

"Sir, I just wanted to give you something unforgettable before you depart from me fore ever.."

She whispered with a wanton look.She swallowed hard and reached out to take his hand. With an easy motion, he withdrew her hand and stood up.

"Why don't you think about Nelson? You are betraying him…" He said, setting his hands on his hips and looking at Ann with a perplexed look on his face.

And why this seduction? This is ridiculous.." He swiveled and went toward the window. He opened the door and peered out on the green lawn. Out side the fence, he could see a herd of cows thudding past an alley, driven by a village boy.

He turned back to her and his eyes seemed cold.

"I am sorry Ann. You are still young and involved with a good relationship. I don't want to spoil it either. It's sin ful. I can't endure the consequences, the wages of sin!

Doctor David went to the door and turned to face her. Something in his taut face told her to let the affair die for ever.

"Ann, we can be just good friends." He said in a cool voice that made her feel the end of explosive chemistry between them. He only offered friendship, a promise beyond which there might be no turnig back in to the past.

"Ann, I hope you would invite me for the betrothal. And,of course, if you invite me for the marriage, I would like to be the best man.." Doctor David said with a hearty laugh.

He regarded her for a moment.

"Of course, I would like to give you a wedding present as well. It's a surprise,can you imagine what it would be?"

He continued laughing, looking at her disheveled elegance in the streaked dark hair,and the shaky fingers scraping through it. There was still a dissappointed expression on her elegant face.

"I am so happy,Sir! certainly I will invite you. After all, you are not a stranger but my close friend! I can't forget you. I have worked for months at your villa,and I have done everything possible to please you.." She smiled a wane smile,wet with tears in her crayfish eyes.

"Thank you Ann, Thank you for giving me the poriority..." Doctor David smiled archly as he groped for the door handle.

Johnson took deep sighs deeply and paced up and down the drawing room. The oldman, imbibed heavily, began to fidget on his chair,grumbling something incoherently and even thinking how he could go to the toaddy shop and get a drink at there. The whisky, he thought, a good damned thing his daughter had bought for him,and his soul was in torment. He loathed his wife,her historical goods and chattles at there tha's so dear for his wife. All his life was obsessed with sins and confined to drinks. His life went happily with playing cards with a group of drunkard friends. He thought about the young gentlemen playing cards in a shady place behind ther toaddy shop, mingled with shouts and idle chatter while playing. May be the stake would be one hundred rupees! But, as for them, it's worth more than the several valuable saddles of the rich! His dreams always confined at there,not on any wonderful soirees arranged in the world,which would accrue to humanity.

The oldman suddenly opened his eyes,wiggled his fingers to portray his ecstacy and added with mime what he could not be added in words. Jhonson broke in to a merry smile,watching him.

Doctor David opened the door and came in,craning his neck, and smiling rapturously at Johnson. Johnson smiled back,stopped pacing about,and walked toward Doctor David.

"My friend, I didn't overhear any worse conversation between Ann and you. Johnson said pressing his index fingers at his ears.

"However, many plans crossed my mind,under this or that article of penal code,against looting and black mailing. But, doctor, it's evident from your rapturous smile that, you have foiled all my schememing of punishment and revenge! And I regret about all those plans crossed in my mind..."

Hearing this, Doctor David cleared his throat awkwardly.

"I am sorry, professor,I should not wish to send Ann in troubles…"

There was a bliss written on Doctor David's face. He seemed so overjoyed and even forgot his antipathy and grudge at Miss. Ann. He came forward and firmly gripped Mr. Johnson's hand.

"I will pull your ears off!" said Johnson with a wide grin as he escorted Doctor David toward the front door.

"Don't you remember? I have told you several times that don't get trapped in her snare! And what's happened? You went shamelessly between her lips, believing her feminine jabber mingled with tears! She could smother you really …"

"Ahem, yes. May be! But, I found her innocent as she confessed. She admitted her crime and said that it all happened under the compulsion of circumstances… And I forgave her." Doctor David looked at Johnson intently,with almost tearful and at the same time exultant eyes.

"Ah, what a plight! you lost in the gamble! you were a fool to believe all of her cooked up story with undue levity…." Johnson mutttered as he walked along with Doctor David. The Doctor, some what disconcerted,smiled sheepishly and tried to turn his attention outside.

A fresh breeze ran over his face. The evening came with a crimson blaze covering a great part of the sky. Over the distance,a soft, warm-looking haze spread out,and the crimson light was shed on the fields,flooded with limpid gold.

Doctor David stepped down the stairs. He sighed with relief and made for the yard. Johnson followed him,raising his eyebrows,and looking sarcastically at his friend.

"I can't believe you. Just tell me one thing. Is it true that you forgave her out of compassion?

"No, I forgave her on reasonable grounds. And,I ask you to postphone the conversation… what's the use of it?"

Johnson grimaced with a feeling that his friend was so faint hearted and a real simpleton. That's why he forgot to take action,that's why he forgot logic with pure compassion to the fair sex. Ann Mary's fabricated lies and her feigned agonizing performance had melted his rage and he went strangely overwrought.He's utterly stupified by her…"

"Well, friend, what's past is past. We cannot bring back all the past that would help us put her under trial. Ah!" Doctor David heaved a sigh, "in the end, I wish, all is best in the world!"

Johnson burst in to a loud laughter. "Yes, friend, past is past,including your fearfully miserable and broken down state! Yes, of course, every misfortune you had to borne with dreadful situations so terrible.." Doctor David blushed like a poopey and kept his eyes fixed on the ground.

Suddenly, the blak hound got up from the shade of a lime tree,and barked convulsively,instantly alarming both of them. They stared at the dog aghast and went shaky on their legs. Somebody had already unfastened it's chain! They went cold all over with fear,got panicky, and ran head long toward the fence. They quickly bounded out in to an alley and ran as swiftly as they could, like two frightened boys. A little more time passed. The barking quickly grew fainter in the distance. Johnson stopped,turned his head back,and kept looking in perplexity,as though he was still expecting the dog in pursuit.

"What are you lookinmg about?" Doctor David asked, panting heavily.

"I am looking for the black hound,snarling and it's red tounge hanging out.." Johnson, chuckled, flinging his head up and drawing a deep breath.

"Heavens! I was scared the hell out of me! Doctor david said in a muffled,apprehensive voice,as if his tounge did not obey him readily.

Panting heavily,and drawing their legs tediously,they walked out of the alley in to an open meadow.A cold breeze wafted across the meadow,diffusing in the soft air the fragrance of autmn aroma. A thin haze hung over the far away green fields,and on the horizon, the sun was set. Heavy masses of storm clouds were still huddled in the distance. The village was before them,with black patches of small cottages huddled together.

Passing across five homesteads,and turning off the right,they discended down a hollow place near the dam. There were peasants moving along the gravelly road near the dam.Several inquisitive glances of passer-by along the road fell over them. They walked toward their parked car at the fence. A thick bush had spread out it's palmated branches over the car. Finally,they got in to the car. Doctor David,moped his perspiring brow, started the car, taking a sharp 'U' turn. He sped cautiously upward the rise. For some minute, he took control of the car over the black trail,as the roaring of the engine grew louder.

An amused grin transformed his face,deepening the lines that webbed his eyes. Half an hour later,he drove the car in to the winding driveway. The driveway was screened either side by tall trees,and verysoon it became deserted. An hour or so passed. As he came before the hill view boulevard, he could see a part of suburb lit up in brilliant lights. In the streams of light, on all sides,everything was sparkling under the falling mist.

Johnson was whistling softly under his breath.,completely relaxed. From time to time, he thumbed his fist in to the palm of his hand.

"My friend, I suppose that we are going to skip the issue.." he grinned at Doctor David.

"That's right. I agree with you.." He shook his head.

"That's good for your sweet heart! My friend, you always accept defeat in a cold manner.."

"It's past. It was just a matter of time!"

Doctor David murmered with coldness in his voice. Out side, it was getting dark with snow drifts in the ravines. A wind was suddenly sprung up, swishing the tree-tops and softly stirring up and driving the fallen,dry leaves on the high way. High up, the moon lit sky seemed magnificent than ever with countless stars,twinkling in rivalary.

CHAPTER 6

ALL BECAUSE OF LUST!

Promptly at seven o' clock Johnson left Doctor David at his home and drove the car toward his villa. He arrived tired, driving in to the porch. He parked the car next to Jame's new, bright red bike.

Nancy was waiting for him concerned. He went in to the hall as she opened the door grim faced. He watched Nancy with a broad grin, finding her dressed in a white cotton dress, off the shoulder.

"You look sensational!" He said. Johnson was careful to make a right note, just to please her. It quickly became obvious to him that Nancy was intend on charming him. But her words were rude.

"Why are you late? It seems that you forget the family. You are running as far away as you could toward.. what shall I say? Yeah, a junkie!"

"Do you think that I am a spoiled kid? A goddamned doped-up kid?" Johnson asked in a rasping whisper. Nancy turned pale and she sighed. It sounded sad and resigned. For a moment, Johnson repented about his inconsiderate words. He began to sound lenient.

"I am sorry, Nancy. I had to spent this afternoon with Doctor David. We did a hell of a job at his house, rearranging, sorting, and stacking his things....."

Nancy smiled as though she found it close to the truth. Before she could respond, Johnson took her and kissed her long and hard. She melted like butter in a hot pan. Slowly, she disengaged, and stepped away toward the kitchen. Before she could slam the kitchen door, Johnson said loudly.

"Darling, I am so tired. I am heading back to the bedroom..."

He laughed low, and tromped toward the stair case, his heavy boots rattling on the ceramic floor. Humming a melodious tune, Johnson climbed the stairs and walked through the corridor. As he stopped and groped for the door handle, he saw Rachel. She was attired in a well-worn swimsuit, doing stretches in an open place on the terrace garden next to the corridor. Her long brown hair tossed from side to side as she worked out. Johnson stood spell bound by her voluptuous body. Her swinging breasts were sweetly rounded and her curly, long hair was glowing in the lamp light.Rachel spread her legs wide and outstretched her hand horizontally.Then she began to move her curvaceous body in to rhythm.Her cleavage was visible through the thin,almost transparant swim suit she wore,and her nipples stood out engorged like two virgin rosebuds.The sight was a source of edndless delight to Johnson.As she danced her way,she had a glimpse of Johnson standing motionless on the corridor a few feet away. They looked at each other and he rather felt a lustful spark leaped from her eyes to him. She giggled and turned around,gazing back over her shoulder.There was a mischeivious grin on her face. Johnson swallowed hard as she showed her shapely bottom to him. He did even think that she was showing her back as if to admire for only to him.

Rachel swung round again to face him,her heavy boobs swaying,and she moved closer to him. Her eyes were dancing up and down on his mascular figure.

"Hello, Johnson." She wished,her raised head in triumph and looking over his face. For a moment, her sparkling eyes traced the lineament of erection on his trousers. A naughty smile broke out on her fabulous face.

"My work out is over. I think it's late. I am going to grab a shower..." Johnson 's nervousness dissolved as she talked more lively and funny. Then she brushed past him with an impish wink.

As Johnson entered his room, his passion was heightened to the edge. Johnson undressed quickly, took a towel, and went in to the bathroom. When he got showered,and began to shake his body, he heard footsteps echoed across the adjoining room.

"Ah, it's Rachel! If I climb a chair and open up the blind slats on the ventilator,I can sure observe her affairs. And if she's going to strip, it would be a sight, and I can watch admiringly at her....." His unseemly thoughts went through a dirty course.

With a spark of daring instinct,johnson went out naked and all wet.He returned soon carrying a deck chair with him. He quickly climbed up the chair and took hold of the blind cord that covered the small window.He put him at ease and yanked it open. The narrow opening was just enough to give him an unobstructed view of the adjoining room. With all anxiety and heart pounding he craned his neck and peered in to the room.

Rachel was standing before the dressing table. Her hair was in a mess, and soft curls matted on her forehead coated with perspiration. Slowly she started taking off her clothes. Off came her swimsuit,her bra, panties and silk garterbelt;everything falling one by one on to the floor. She stook stark naked and looked in to the mirror as if to check her out. Slowly she began to stroke her breasts and weighed their heaviness in her cupped palms. She sighed,her eyes flashing a wanton look.

Her body was soft and full with well-rounded breasts.Her curves were equisite and that set a standard.Her eyes had a far away look,but it remained sweet and seductive. Rachel turned and crossed the room buck naked,her round ass flexing as she walked,and nicely showing it off to Johnson. An exultant look developed on her face and her sparkling eyes darted for a moment at the ventilator. Johnson could hardly control himself and he watched her breathless. Long,soft brown curls neatly framed her classic looks! She looked like a beautiful geisha expecting to be rewarded. She smiled for a moment at the ventilator and then looked away.

Johnson turned his attention to the gorgeous brown mink framed between her lovely thighs. A fierce desire for her body made his blood course swiftly through his body.

Rachel leaned toward a desk and switched on a stereo-system. As the tempo of the music increased,she shrugged her shoulders sensuously and began to dance. Still swaying to the music,she then began to give a show,apparently unconcerned that somebody was watching! Her eyes were closed as she continued swaying her hips in a sensual rhythm. Immediately the dance grew in to a variety of slow, sexy numbers.

Johnson squinted his eyes and watched dazed at the slight parting of her creamy thighs signalling arousal.Her whole figure was exotic, overwhelmingly erotic and he was really panting with desire..

Suddenly a yellow fly flew in to his bathroom through the narrow opening of the ventilator and hung suspended above Johnson's head. The exquisite pleasure of voyeurism had already knocked all other thoughts out of his mind and he was in utter daze. He didn't see or listen the fly buzzing above his head in circular motion. His fingers were still dug on the blind slats and his eyes never left on her womanly charms! Sweat broke out on his forehead and suddenly he had a burgeoning erection rising from the bed of his wiry hair.

Meanwhile, the yellow fly fluttered round his body and slowly alighted down. All of a sudden, the fly settled round his heavy balls and buried it's sting in to his flesh. And before Johnson waved his left hand uneasily, the fly darted away with a droning sound. With a loitering motion the fly disappeared out of the bathroom.

"A..a..a..aaa..!" Johnson gave a rasping cry, rubbing his balls with a wet hand The first thing he sensed clearly was an acute pain spreading over his balls. He jumped down the chair, kicked out one leg in pain, and burst out crying in a nastily squealing note.

Johnson ran in to the bedroom and sat heavily on the edge, examining his swollen balls. A horrible sensation ran down the length of his body. Through his incessant wailing cries, he imagined that a piece of crackers had blown up his balls. He also had a horrible feeling that his genitals, legs and everything had been ripped away from his body. His face was so grave and his eyes dazzled. Everyminute, he fearfully fancied that death was nigh, had come closer, that his heart would stop beating. He abruptly took a pillow and coverded it over his genitals. Pressing the pillow hard with both hands, and again bursting in to tears he called nancy vociferously with a ghastly contorted face.

Nancy and James rushed in to his room almost together. As they stared at johnson in amazement, the first thing they noticed was a shaking Johnson as if caught with fever, and his eyes bulged, siezed with an overwhelming horror. He was also waving his arms about helplessly, and crying by the first paroxysm of extreme pain.

"Nancy, my darling! I am terrified.. I am terrified!" He muttered, still shaking with fright and he gave both of them a dismayed look. Pressing the pillow over his genitals he sank helplessly on to the bed.

"Nancy," He whimperd, "I am dying! Save me please!" He moved his loin agonizingly.

James glanced in perplexity now and again at Johnson's naked body and the pillow that covered his mid section.

"Johnson, dear! What's happened? Why cry, really? Are you unwell? I will call the doctor…" Nancy whimperd through her tears. She bent down and tried to pull his hands away from the pillow. To make the situation more awkward and completely at a loss for words,Johnson grunted and waved her back. Nancy looked at him quizzically.

"Oh, Nancy! Please don't dare to take the pillow away. Now it's my only consolation!" He mumbled as the wild music in the adjoining room grew all the wilder.

"I can't understand you, Johnson. Take that pillow away and get dressed. If you feel terribly sick, I will call Doctor David.." Nancy said in a faint voice.

Johnson passed a trembling hand over his forehead and wiped the sweat.

"Look Nancy, the problem is right down there.."He pointed his index finger at his loin. Then he leaned closer to her and began to explain the appalling news in sibilant whisper.

"Listen to me Nancy, I am telling you quite seriously that I am going to die soon! You know a yellow wasp kissed my balls while I got showered. ..."

Nancy heard him out,narrowing her eyes,and she slowly pulled the edge of the pillow.Johnson felt unbearably ashamed as she examined his swollen testicle with her hand. The grave preoccuppied expression on her face was enhanced by the terrible sight.

James was standing near by. He swept a glance out of the corner of his eyes and suddenly burst in to a hysterical laughing.

"You swine! Why are you laughing? Johnson grunted, irritation ebbing his eyes.

James stopped laughing,and looked regretfully at Johnson's face distorted with anger.

He expressed sorry to make mock at his uncle's deplorable state.He hastened to the telephone and said seriously.

"I am sorry. I will call Doctor David and explain..."

Johnson pulled the blanket over his body,curled up and began to collect the images of Rachel. What a woman she is! A seducing witch? He began to recollect the events he spent together with her. All those events flickered in his imagination in to a single whole. But they simply refused to be assembled,although she was hot,so close and he wanted her badly.So bady to take her over the edge of erotic pleasure!

As johnson began to shiver and gasp under the blanket, Nancy slid her down his belly and slowly caressed his pudenta.It felt so hot and puffy!

"I am an idiot! what a stupid fool a man must be not to find satisfaction with his beautiful wife!"

Johnson thought regretfully,with out tearing his eyes away from his wife's tear stained face. And this thought remained with him even in his sleep.

A short while later,Doctor David's car drove up and pulled up precisely near the porch.James trotted speedily to the front door and received him cordially.

"James, tell me what's his condition? He was very fine a few hours ago with me ..."

Doctor david asked, blinking his eyes in amazement.

"It seems that his condition is terrible.." James replied,clearing his throat, as he ushered the Doctor in.

"Well, it was a difficult drive in the dark night with the smoking fog and huge black shadows all the way round..." Doctor David muttered as he climbed the stairs.

Doctor David announced his arrival with a cough as he entered the bed room,his glossy boot creaking loud enough for the whole house to hear. Nancy wiped her tears and went to meet the Doctor. Wringing her hands before him,she explained her husband's situation in a drawling note like a prosodist.

Doctor David rushed to the head of the bed and roused Johnson from his sleep. Then he pulled the blanket off and began to examine his patient.

Nancy went up to him and asked with a sinking heart.

"Doctor,he's not in any danger,is he?"

"I don't think so" He chuckled,while he wrote prescription and handed it over to her.

"The patient has only little problem.He's suffering general anxiety mingled with pain and fatigue.Don't worry. It's after all, a silly case of bee bite.."

He leaned forward with a bright smile,opened his box and rummaged for the contents.All the while he looked over Johnson and muttered words enough to console him. He took out a bottle of Antiseptic solution and sponge and turned to Johnson. Then he totally focussed on Johnson's swollen balls and began to scrub the solution gently over it. Johnson felt tickles for a moment.

"Ah! Thank you Doctor,you are the third one caressing my balls. The first one is me,the second my wife and the third...!" He burst in to laughter.

"Doctor,now I can really feel the divine wrath.." Johnson mumbled as the Doctor looked at him quizzically.

"What do you mean?" He raised a brow.

"The wages of sin!"

Doictor David grinned ear to ear and blurted out.

"Hell! Look like we sinners get in there just in time simultaneously.Well, tell me all about the sinful deeds later."

There was still a wide grin on Dotor David's face as he took out a syringe.

He injected anti dote just below on Johnson's shoulder as he took a deep breath.

Doctor David turned to Nancy.

"He's going to make it and take care of him. With in hours,you could see the vital signs of slow recuperation."He assured her, "He's going to be fine."

Then he turned and bent down,whispering in Johnson's ear.

"Don't worry friend. I hope that within three days your wings would sprout from the base.You have to wait patiently for a burgeoining erection. Always keep up brightest hopes!"

Doctor David patted on his shoulder and went out with a satisfied mien, followed by james,carrying his box.

Johnson leaned back comfortably on the pillow placed on the headboard.

"Johnson, do you feel relaxed? I think the pain would subside soon. Everything will turn alright soon..." Nancy said with a broad smile, her twinkling eyes resting on his face. Johnson recollected that since his betrothal,he had found her a perfect match, and he was very happy. She had embodied every women of virtues and qualities he had ever dreamed up. And before marriage,he often rolled her name on his tounge,remembering her smiling face and twinkling eyes. She was used to wear nice dresses,crumbled in deep folds at the waist. And he cherished to dream about her, even while lying on his lonely bed in the wee hours of morning. She was then a beautiful girl of twenty one,endowed with tastes and temperament similar to him, and also with instincts of beauty. He was instantly attracted to her, and her intriguing nature, her carelessness that lend a peculiar charm to her personality.

"Johnson, what are you thinking?" Nancy asked in a sing song voice, shuffling and then caressing his hair gently.

Johnson ripped himself from his vivid memories,and looked at his wife with an affable look.

"Darling, I was thinking about the past. How speedily time went in leaps and bounds! I have told you several times that I have never had a love affair in my life until I saw you. Not a single romantic adventure in the whole of my life. When we got betrothed, I became absolutely changed,enjoying the love of you.

I enjoyed the thrill of secret rendezvous at dimlit rooms of restaurants,theatres and shady parks. I could almost feel all those excitement of love affair,such things as trysts,lovers sighing,hot kisses and fondling. I sensed and enjoyed the euphoria of wanton love. But, today in my deteriorated condition and cooped up in my bedroom, I am thinking of the past,reviving one after the other in my memory..."

There was a tinge of gloom in his words. But a look at nancy's elegant profile made him smile fondly. Nancy clasped his hand,raised it to the side of her face and gently imprinted a kiss on it.

"Nancy, do you remember how the two of us went on horseback down the valley to visit an old church? And how we spent together the whole night in a large,almost dilapidated,damp house? It was a clear day when we set out,and suddenly the rain fell in torrents with a violent wind suddenly roared overhead. We were all drenched up and shivering and when the horse began to stumble on the slippery ground,we were forced to stop it. We dismounted briskly and huddled close to a spreading bush.For some time we crouched down and covered our faces.We waited patiently for the storm to blow over. It was towards evening. After sometime the rain and wind ceased and everything went quiet and calm. I quickly got and went up to the horse sheltered under a branch. I took the bridle,pulled her up and guided her along the way. After trudging with difficulty through the mud,we decided to mount on the horseback. Suddenly you showed me an abandoned house,hovering like a ghost house in the slight drizzle before our very eyes. It was surrounded by a high fence round the dense forest. We moved toward there,hoping for somebody to help us. But the house was deserted and we stayed a whole night at there. We chatted the whole night, crouching before the burning logs we made,watching the fire flickering up and dying mournfully. It was a terrible night........"

"Johnson you recollect all the events vivdly as if it all had happened a few months ago. Yes, johnson I can also recollect that night under a damp, moscovered wooden cieiling. The house was a terrible place and I was really scared whenever I heard a shrill, and plaintive voice broke up the profound silence. I huddled close to you almost trembling and you laughed at me.You tried to assure me that it's the sound of a toad lurching under the mud.Suddenly from out of the distance came a prolonged,resonant,almost wailing sound. I was totally grieved and I began to weep like a child. You again laughed, poking the fire with a stick,and consoled me that it's storm gathering in the woods.

The sound rose up on the air,lingered and then slowly died away. But I got a terrible fright again and began to say, 'it's dark every where except this place. Johnson, now suppose the ghosts were to come..' And before I had fininshed saying this, some one suddenly walked above our heads.For some time we listened the stranger walking upstairs. We could see the wooden boards jerking intermittantly as the ghost crossed over.We exchanged frightened glances and I screamed in horror, 'Johnson, this is a haunted place! Christ be with us!' And I made a sign of the cross. I was scared stiff and I had a sensation of fainting. I fell over your shoulders and hugged you tightly.

'Funny!' you said after a brief silence,and again listening to the sound overhead.

'I can imagine that it's a bundicoot scurriying over there.' But it was no good for me in a derilict,scarry place.....''

Nancy paused,gazing at Johnson with maudlin affection. Johnson laughed.

"Nancy, I could imagine what's going on in your heart just then", He said,egging himself on with memories, "So, I decided to wipe out your terrible fright and superstitious misgivings about supernatural elements.I began to talk to you a lot,particularly about some psychological reasons for your fright on ghosts and spirits. I was still grinning,watching your lithe form soaked in mud and rain. Then I closely watched your terrified face and began to rub along the inside of your thighs. Then I said with a wink, 'you get so upset about a scarry night.What about getting laid? I am sure it would relax your tension...' Your eyes were closed,tears trickling down. Suddenly you opened your eyes and stared at me with an embarassed look.I moved closely and pulled up your skirt. As the dress tantalizingly ascended,I could see you covering your face with evident shame. I began to request and you immediately complied. My fingers traced a light path above your shapely legs.And you shivered and mumbled in a voice deep in your throat, 'Johnson, is it right to get laid before the marriage?' All I could do was to emit a growl as I moved between your legs. Quickly I began my first thrust,but before I reached you there, I froze and yelled at the top of my voice. I was scared at the sight of a centipede creeping over your tight halter top. I literally jumped back,and stuffed my thing abruptly inside my fly. I regret that I couldn't fuck you right then..."

Nancy burst into peals of laughter,and held his head in her arms.

"Johnson,I think it was your first coitus interruption! You were always like a child,scared of reptiles, stinging flys and beetles. You have to be bold enough to shed that kind of phobia. Well, Johnson, as for me you were a good husband, so kind and warm that, after the marriage, we could maintain a very vigorous sex life. But still, I am sorry Jhonson! I couldn't give you a fantastic parting gift to your bachelorhood that night........"

Nancy was sitting groggily, her mind suddenly clouded by sleep. She looked at the clock. Half past nine. She stood up tired, half asleep and then straightened out. She mumbled after a yawn.

"Johnson, it's getting late. I am going to the dining room. I will return, bringing your supper..."

Nancy walked toward the door, swaying sleepily from side to side, and shuffled her way out of the room.

A minute passed in silence. Johnson lay comfortably on the bed and glanced with delight at the glass window gilded by the moonlight. He listened to the sound of a small bat fluttering across the window in a loitering motion. Then he heard spike heels echoing on the corridor. Suddenly, to his enormous surprise, Rachel appeared on the doorway with a charming smile on her face. She was wearing a pair of cut-off jeans and a dark blue Tshirt that clung to her breasts like a second skin.

"How do you feel Johnson?" She glanced inquiringly at him and stood motionless, closing the door and leaning against the doorjamb.

Johnson watched her in amazement. He tried to speak, but he could only keep moving his lips, and no words came out. Then he nodded his head numbly and stared at her, as she walked over to the bed.

She breathed so heavily, standing at the bed side and slowly pulled a chair toward the head of the bed. Johnson remained stolidly silent as she sat on the chair at the side of the bed. Sitting on the edge of the chair, she spread her legs wide and gazed down at him sympathetically. She reached out a hand and clasped his wrist. Johnson tingled as she caressed his palm and began to squeeze his fingers gently. He looked at her shining eyes, which he thought, had a tint of mischief. Some how he mustered up the energy to speak.

"Rachel, you wouldn't believe it! You know, an hour ago a yellow fly flew in, arched it's back, and stung me mercilessly. The nast creature! Now I am in a miserable condition, suffering pain and quite enfeebled...."

"Oh, I can hardly believe it! How unfortunate you are.. it's terrible!" She bent down and crooned softly in his ear. Her flowing hair caressed his face. Her proximity aroused so much pleasure and he had a giddy sense of her musky aroma flowing in to his nostrils. Johnson inhaled loudly and let out a long breath,throwing his head back on the pillow.

Rachel rose up with a seductive smile and watched his face silently,flushed with emotion. She leaned closer across the bed side table and whispered.

"Johnson, I know you are attracted to me! But, you can't imagine how worse is my situation. At first, I can't reconcile with your childish demeanor obsessed with sex. You were watching me with lust like every fucking guy in the world wants to lay me! For some days, I couldn't believe your incredible change,and frolicsome behaviour.It kind of things numbs things out! Why don't you realize my situation? You are a respectable person, and besides, a person married to my best friend...."

Johnson raised himself up and leaned his head on the head board. He stared stunned at her words,and jolted wide awake from his half sleep. Rachel continued her hoarse mumble,waving her arms about.

"I heard you were the best person ever found from Nancy.I have been thinking respectfully ever since I acquainted with you. But you changed my attitude completely. It' s because you were finding for chances to get alone with me,just to behave frivolously.You have been been behaving so wanton,fraught with lust as if trying for an opportunity to try to get in my pants. It came as kind of a shock to me...."

Johnson moved his body to her side and grasped her hand.He mumbled as though he couldn't resist her carnal charms.

"Rachel! it's because you are the most beautiful woman I have ever laid eyes on!"

Rachel started and looked at his face in shock. She could feel the unbridled,aggressive desire for sex smoldering in his eyes. He was staring at her breasts and looking from there to her waist. She pulled away his hand and sat down on the chair disgusted. Her face reddened with anger and quikly she spread her knees apart.

"Like what you see? What's this Johnson. You are again behaving like a nerd ..."

Ashamed of her muttering,he turned his head away from her side and fell silent. He was avoiding his face from her, asthough he won't let her see the foolish, guilty and strained look on it. Rachel suddenly turned pale with a feeling of remorse and her head drooped.

"I am sorry Johnson,for all the things that turned round like this. It's my fate! I can fathom your love,your lust and everything to me. But I am helpless. I cannot force myself to fall in love!"

Johnson turned his head with a dismayed look and studied her face. He could see an uneasy feeling came over her fabulous face.

"Johnson I can't believe what's happening to me! You know, at first I thought your connection was just an annoyance,but gradually it became clear to me that I am also feeling the same passion toward you. I have been enjoying your presence,and I began to revel in this new found passion with clandestine desires. I confess, I had been thrown against my will in to this amourette.This mounting desire began to annoy me greatly and with a strange feeling of frustration as well. The wistful, warm, sentimental mood inspired by the person,the husband of my best friend,made me guilty. This relationship warned me that I am cheating my best friend. I can't bear this feeling of guilt,that prick at my conscience,any more. That's why I decide to leave this place tomorrow. You may think it strange and obstinate. But I don'r care.. The situation is terrible…."

Rachel whispered with a feeling of pain flitted across her face,and heaved a sigh.

"And what if I won't let you go?" Johnson mumbled with an agonized look on his face. Rachel smiled.

"You have to let me go. It's customary for guests to depart whenever they decide." She moved closer to him and again whispered in to his ear with a sweet,tremulous voice.

"Johnson, there's no knowing what was to blame for my foolishness! And I know you were watching me greedily through the bathroom window. You have been watching my prank,while I stripped and danced in nude. Do you know, it's the only thing I could show you as if a touching farewell! keep up the scene in your mind! Because I am helpless,and I can't do anything for you except that exhibition of madness…….."

A full blown smile came over her face as she looked coyly at Johnson. Then she laughed merrily. Johnson's eyes were wide with surprise and his mouth fell open.

"Okay, I have confessed my love and everything to you before I leave. Now I feel relieved and happy. Tomorrow,at seven o' clock sharp, I will leave your house. Before leaving,I want to inform you some personal matter. You know, my parents are already cheered up,having fixed up an arranged marriage for me.Like every parents,they had designs on my person. They were on the look out for an eligible suiter sofar.And much to my surprise, they found a suitable one, a soft ware engineer working at USA. My parents called me yesterday and insisted to return as soon as possible…"

"Well, I am so happy. You let me understand your feeling and how calmly you had covered it up with a blithe complacensy before me. Thank you for your frankness. And if you find me faulty, I apologize for the mistakes I have done to you…" Johnson paused for a moment,looking in to her eyes with a strange sense of loss.

"Rachel,darling, what shall I say when you are going away from me? Any way, I wish you a happy journey. I think that your parents have got a best proposition for you.Wish you all the best!"

Johnson's eyes were welled up with tears. His face turned pale,and his lips were trembling.

With a scarcely perceptible flutter of her long eyelashes, Rachel reached for his hand and sat down beside him on the bed.

"Thank you,Johnson. You will be always a good friend of me…"

Johnson secretly pressed her palm, and each time he pressed it she gave him a friendly smile. Slowly,he lowered her against the pillow on the bed,his weight pressing her deeper.

"No, Johnson!"Rachel uttered a squealy note. But she couldn't resist his abrupt movements. His hands quickly explored her soft curves,inhibited by the T shirt.A fluttering tumult of desire left her breath loud and quick. His hands glided slowly over her stomach,creating new dimensions of arousal. His hand went farther down. The contact of a gentle palm over her pubic mound stimulated her own needs unaware.

Johnson took her head in his trembling hands and bent down his head. His mouth found hers and he kissed her hard and fast,his tounge thrusting inside with a preview of uncontrollable passion.

"No! We shouldn't do this!" Rachel breathed heavily,breaking free of his mouth. A deep groan escaped from his mouth with evident dissapointment. Rachel quikly pulled his hands away and got up. She was shivering as if in a fever. Both of their eyes met in stricken expressions. Rachel suddenly emitted a cry. It was followed by a heavy shuddering sigh. There was a pleading expression on her face.

"You don't expect me to do this, Johnson! It's cheating! let me go " She swiveled and went to the door. She opened the door and peered out in to the corridor.Then she turned to him and straightened her flowing hair. Sudddenly an amused grin transformed her face,and she said loudly.

"Good night, Johnson. See you tomorrow!"

A pensive cloud of despair fell over Johnson's eyes as she left him with out a backward glance.

Out side the window, the night was enfolding everything in a gentle soporific embrace. Only a night bird drawled out a lazy, long and articulate sound.

EPILOGUE

It was early morning, slightly wet with the mist. A sudden gust of wind wafted across the street and swirled away whirling eddies of dust along the road. The eastern mountain peaks, and the horizon extended far and wide, were flodded with crimson. The morning sun was slowly rising. Farther away down the street, the valley was still clouded with a heavy fog. The trees along the road were shaking their naked branches in the wind. All the birds were whistling and twittering.

It was a Sunday morning. Sophia was busy with her morning routine, which send her on the way to a comfortable life style. She went up stairs and roused Doctor David from his sleep. She smiled at her father and handed him a steaming cup of bed coffee. Then she shuffled her way out and hurriedly went downstairs. She was getting all ready for her morning run marathons up the hills. Then, after a while, she had to serve her duties as a young member on the board of directors of the church, and also participate to sing in the choir.

Her two storeyed house was situated in a quiet place, overlooking a lake with park on the other side. Sophia went outside and came down the porch to pick up the newspaper. She was a petite brunette endowed with small, supple breasts. She was wearing a tight stretch pants and a blue, flannel turtle neck shirt. Long, wavy brown hair framed her pretty face with minimal makeup. The tight stretch pants she was wearing showed of her sexy legs, which had underneat it, the kind of long, tight runners muscles. She had an ass, for sure, firm, tight and round. Her habit of running up hills had kept her ass sagging.

Sophia spent a short time, reclining on the lounge chair, reading the news paper headlines. Then she set out for her running marathons, occasionally nodding and greeting the familiar passers-by. There were enough joggers for her, coming out in stream from the neighbourhood and also some biginners. Sophia got together with a group of familiar neighbours and went on regular hiking on the road. They were loudly chatting something on their measured strides.

The lake side was clothed with rows of sentinel trees. On the opposite side of the lake, the hilly bank was dotted with peasants small cottages,and a greater part was bounded by green meadows.

Half an hour later,Sophia was running alone swiftly across a narrow track. She forced her way across the edge of a tea estate.She was panting heavily and sprinting with feverish rapidity. While hiking up, she surveyed all round. A split second later,something sailed past her head and crashed on the branches of a tall tree. She stopped at once in amazement and looked up to see what it was. The high way above was empty. Ther was only the distant roar of the engine of a truck. Who ever threw the thing was gone! Still looking on the road above, she tried not to panic.

Shophia stopped hiking and slowly climbed a slope,occasionally parting the bushes with her hands. The green path on the slope was dappled with shadows in the sunlight. A fresh breeze ran over her face as she clambered up and arrived at the road. The sun was rising up,but shedding no warmth. She glanced around and saw everything green under the lifting mist.

Suddenly, somebody roared along the road on a motorcycle,hurtling a bump,with the wheels spinning faster with a jump. The crazy cool guy riding the bike dangerously,waved a hand to Sophia and began to circle around her,standing in the middle of the road. Sophia inturn, her face flushed with rage,held up her hand to stop him. The rider stopped the bike and hopped off with a broad grin. He quickly pulled off his helmet and pointed toward a leafy branch down the road.

"Hey, did you hear something crashed out down there a short while ago?

Sophia scowled her face, "Yeah, I could hear the sound. I can figure it out now! You scamp!"

Sophia gazed deepily in to the rider's eyes,savouring memories.He was also staring at her,never moving his mischievious eyes from her beautiful face. The sweat was streaming in rivulets down her elegant face.

"Sophia, glad to meet you." He said in an excited and overjoyed voice.

"I am delighted to meet you, James. A pleasure!"

She offered james a sweaty hand. After this came a prolonged handshake,hile he peered intently in to her sparkling eyes. A smile broke out on her face.

"Well, James,you scared me terrible,throwing a brick or something down over there!" Sophia said,feeling her hand warmed up in his grip.

"I am thinking to start kick your ass.." She said,pulling away her hand from his.

After a few minutes chit chat Sophia suggested for a drive back toward her house. James nodded his head with a smile and jumped on the bike.As he revved the bike Sophis slid behind the back seat.He took off,riding slowly down the bent road.

"Sophia, I am worried about how to establish a relationship with a girl ..." He said, driving slowly down the highest point of the curve that must be one hundred feet high.

"Don't worry, James. Let's talk to her together.." Sophia said, blushing slightly. She huddled closely to his back,hugging him tightly. James felt her hot breath on his neck. He began to feel happiness,and a new sensation of sweetnes and hot.

"But, sophia, she's a total freak! You know, she 's a choir girl and very busy about the church affairs." He said,looking back over his shoulder for a moment. He heard her exclaim loudly. Then he felt her hands creeping over his shoulder.All atonce he felt a scratch like with that of the rough paws of a cat.

"Nonsense!" She yelled as if she had lost her temper.

"It's not nonsense. I am quite serious.." He whimpered,feeling with pain on his shoulders.

"Rubbish! I'd advise you to stop acting the fool ..." She said loudly.

James laughed and let his left hand fall on her thigh.He slowly played with his fingers while she trembled, then he felt a slight pull on his hand.

"James,you are really crazy!" He heard her giggling. A happy sound in the wake of a shallow breath!

"Ah, she's biting.." Whispered James,trembling with imaptience.

"Sophia,tell me what's your conception of an eligible suiter?" He asked, getting up enough momentum to ride downwards.

"Well, I should like to marry a writer. He should write poems all the time.." She mumbled.

"Oh, if it is poems you want, I can write them for you.."

"What can you write about?" she again giggled.

"About love,feelings..your crayfish eyes.. your sweet red lips... Iam sure it will drive you crazy.."

Sophia burst in to a loud laughter. James exerted in to high gear and raced up at full speed. After driving along a down ward curve,he stopped the bike on hig place grown up with several pine woods.They jumped down the bike and looked round. It was a deserted place. From their feet down to the bottom ran a slope toward a water's edge,which the sun gazing down in to it like a mirror.

James rubbed his hands and said.

"Do let's slide down the slope,sophia. Just once!", He pleaded, "I assure you we will be quite safe and sound..."

Sophia was really afraid. Her heart sank at the mere sight of the slope. What would happen if she were to risk plunging in to deep water?"

"Don't be afraid. I beg you! If you deny,it would be faint hearted,cowardly, don't you see?"

Sophia heaved a sigh and finally relented. They climbed on to the bike. James crooned a song and revved up the bike.He spun round the open place twice and kept right on going. Then,before Sophia warned him he's risking their lives, he drove down the curve.Sophia,closed her eyes,put her arms round his waist and hugged him tighly. The bike whizzed off like a bullet through the air lower and lower,swerving and wobbling in wild momentum.

"I love you Sophia!" James whispered quietly. Sophia heard him,but she was more dead than alive,pale and hardly breathing.

"I love you Sophia!" James screamed against the roar of the wind and the rumble of the vehicle.

As they finally reached the bottom, james pulled up precisely with an easy motion. He turned his face to her,smiled and shrugged.

"Oh, my God! I wouldn't go down again for anything!" Sophia said,trembling slightly and looking at James with wide, horror-striken eyes. "I nearly died!"

They jumped off the bike and looked at each other. Sophia recovered her senses and began looking in to his eyes enquiringly.

"Did you say those four words?" She asked as if the puzzle of the words gave her no peace.

"Yes, the four words that indicate my love. You know, I don't want to hide my feelings.And I said 'I love you Sophia!'

She looked at James under her lashes, understanding him. Sophia smiled, put her arm through him and they walked along the waters edge. Sophia kept darting at him questioning glances while she answered his several doubts absent mindedly. There was still a play of strong emotions on her dear face!

Finally,they stopped before a wonderful spot near the waters edge, between dens clumps of riverside bushes. They descended down hand in hand and sat down together on the ground.

"I am glad we are alone atlast!' He began,looking round.

"I have a lot to say to you, Sophia. A great deal. When I saw you for the first time at the church hall, I fell in love at first sight. Yes, believe me, I fell passionately in love!"

Sophia looked up at his flushed face and her insides ached for normalcy. His voice imprisoned her heart,and his kind eyes tamed her soul.

"James, are you serious? You love me? I can't believe this. I was used to get hear it from other boys quite so foolishly..." Her brow arched with amusement.

James dropped his hand on her shoulder,and slowly slid it down her arm.

"I don't want to seem too obvious. I only knew onething that I love you and I need you, Sophia..." He took her arm and lowered his face.She closed her eyes as if a token of assent and let him kiss on her hand.

"James, love didn't come that easily. I am not thinking about a relationship right now. But you are offering it to me. What shall I say?" She sighed heavily.

A gust of wind slapped her hair against his face.James moved closely and took her in his arms, enclosing her in his arms. His face was inches away from hers,and she could smell the clean scent of his after-shave.She smiled up at him, convinced that the explosive chemistry between them had been developing beyond mere friendship. The movement of his fingers was hypnotizing,and her heart fluttered against her rib cage as she felt his face brushing her cheeks. Suddenly he framed her face with both hands and moved down his head.His lips touched her fore head,her eyes and he began trailing tiny kisses down her cheeks

"I love you, Sophia. Love me!" He whispered.

"You don't know what's my position!" She exclaimed against him.

"I am intoxicated!" He explained against her soft cheek and dropped a kiss on her trembling lips.

"So, will you marry me?" She looked up in to his warm, moist eyes and saw he was serious.

"Yes." His gasp sent her in to an astonished stare.

"I am serious about making you my wife." He whimpered again.A crystal tear escaped from his eyes and dropped on to her cheek.

"Well, let my father consider your proposition!" She laughed as he lowered her against the ground. His rough hand stole under her soaked sweater,while he looked at her with hooded eyes,opaque with entreaty.He needed that innocence and wonder as much as he'd needed anything in his life!

Sophia's fingers crawled up his chest. She panted heavily. Nothing in her past,no experience with men,had prepared her for this.The sweet,overwhelming desire fired new blazes through her,until the ache inside her was ubearable.

Sophia gasped in quick breaths and began to respond to his need with an unaccountable joy filled her yearning soul.

A fresh wind slowly stirred up and drove dry leaves over her rolling bodies. They were not prepared to listen anything. There was only a new melody with hot kisses and sighs while they made love, crossing the threshold of pleasure. The love making, the exhilaration and the aftermath were actually beyond imagination.

And it's a fact that nothing could battle the urge of youthful energies,desires and instincts for the boldest exploration with which they cross adventurous frontiers!

Mean while, the early sun rose higher with brilliance,and everything was fresh, gay and delightful. Below the sun, the blue ripples whisked gladly along the river,lifting rhythmically a canoe rowing diagonally upstream.